One man had already used Gayle because of her father's position. She refused to let Landon do the same thing.

Gayle paused and took a drink of iced tea. Landon remained quiet, willing her to go on.

"My father is Evert Johnson, governor of Kentucky. He's been in public service since I was small. I've campaigned for him and I worked in his administration before I came here."

Landon reached over and took her hand. . . .

"I know," he said.

"You know?" Gayles said in a quiet voice. "You know?" She said loder this time.

"I found out while working on my book. I sent a questionnaire to him, which I'm sure you remember answering. That's why you read my books. I didn't make the connection when I first met you. It was only later. . . that I saw your picture with him in an article."

"You know all about me and my family?" Gayle asked.

"I read all the articles about your father and many about you. The *Redbook* article was impressive. Your dad is quite the politician. He'll win that Senate seat."

"I see. So, have you made your selection for your book?" She asked in a tight voice.

"Not yet. That dependes on you. Your father is our number one choice."

I want you to leave, Landon. Right now," she said in an icy voice.

"But Gayle," Landon protested. "You don't understand."

"I understand all I need to know. And don't call me Gayle. I'm Ginny."

VEDA BOYD JONES writes romances "that confirm my own values." Jones lives with her husband, an architect, and three sons in the Ozarks of Missouri.

Books by Veda Boyd Jones

HEARTSONG PRESENTS

HP21—Gentle Persuasion
HP35—Under a Texas Sky

The Governor's Daughter

Veda Boyd Jones

Heartsong Presents

*For Cathy Kellough and Lillian Watt, for pointing
me in the right direction.*

Thanks to Jimmie, Landon, Morgan, and
Marshall for walking all those precinct
blocks as we learned about the political
process.

ISBN 1-55748-435-X

THE GOVERNOR'S DAUGHTER

Copyright © 1993 by Veda Boyd Jones. All rights reserved.
Except for use in any review, the reproduction or utilization of
this work in whole or in part in any form by any electronic,
mechanical, or other means, now known or hereafter invented,
is forbidden without the permission of the publisher, Heartsong
Presents, P.O. Box 719, Uhrichsville, Ohio 44683.

PRINTED IN THE U.S.A.

one

Her first job interview. And under false pretenses, too. Did she really want to make the switch from privileged daughter to unknown office worker?

Virginia Gayle Johnson's soft face hardened with determination as she looked out the office window at the dismal January day. The snow that had been gloriously white coming down two days before was now heaped dingy brown beside the campus sidewalks. She shifted in the hard chair, her cobalt blue eyes returning to the little gray-haired man behind the large desk studying her application.

"Miss Johnson, your typing ability surpasses the requirement by our employment office, and that's the main function of the department secretary. That and knowing how to operate a computer. You do realize the job is only temporary, just this spring semester?"

"Yes," Gayle said and nodded.

"Sharon is taking an extended maternity leave and actually hadn't planned on leaving until after semester enrollment was over." He leaned back in his chair and chuckled. "But you just can't time when little ones want to jump into the world."

"Then your secretary has already had her baby?" Gayle asked, warming to the pleasant tone in Dr. Webber's voice.

"Last night. A little boy, six pounds something. I just called the job over to the employment office this morning and didn't expect them to move so fast. Guess you happened to be in the right place at the right time." His voice seemed to hold a question.

"Yes, I suppose so," Gayle replied noncommittally. She didn't want to supply any more facts about herself and why she was interested in a temporary job. She hadn't lied on her application, she had merely stopped short of mentioning her full name or that she was a graduate of Harvard Law School.

"I think you will do very well here," Dr. Webber said. "Perhaps another position will open up after this semester, and you could move into it." Again she had the idea he was waiting for her to say something, but she remained quiet. "How soon can you start?"

"Tomorrow, sir," Gayle stated.

"Splendid. Hours are seven-thirty until four-thirty with an hour off for lunch. Since our first classes start at eight, many of the professors need some quick typing done before then. Of course, classes won't be in session again until next week, but enrollment begins Wednesday. Tomorrow will give you a day to get familiar with the routine before the students hit you with problems.

"Well," Dr. Webber added as he stood, announcing the end of the interview, "if you've no further questions, I'll see you tomorrow."

Gayle picked up her heavy coat and held it over her arm, shook hands with Dr. Webber, and walked out, smiling to herself.

She had a job. It was a first step in her quest for independence. "Thank You, Lord," she whispered as she stopped in the hall and shrugged into her coat. She stepped out into the bitterly cold wind and pulled the collar up around her neck. Her friend, Marta, had assured her that this was an exceptional cold spell, that temperatures in northern Arkansas didn't linger around the zero mark for long.

Gayle walked quickly toward the parking lot, which was nearly empty since the students were still on semester break. The only activity was a tall, blond man who was locking his car. He turned and walked toward her. As they came abreast she glanced into dark gray eyes and murmured a friendly, "Hi," which was returned with a deep masculine voice and an appreciative smile. Gayle continued past two more cars until she reached hers, then turned back to look again and saw that he was turning for a second look himself. She raised her hand in a parting wave, and he returned the salute.

Ah, she thought as she drove toward Marta's combination house and craft store, *so I am not immune to the opposite sex after all. Maybe back in the hidden recesses of my mind I had doubts about Frank all along.*

That was a novel idea, and she mused about it, letting her mind travel back to that December day in Kentucky. She had left Frankfort early to drive into Lexington and had walked into Frank's outer office. His secretary, Althea, hadn't been at her desk, and the door to the inner office was ajar. Frank's deep laugh had floated out, and she had smiled as she'd walked toward the office, figuring he was in a good mood and as eager for their evening date as she was. Three steps from the door she had been stopped short by Althea's seductive tones.

"Darling, will I see you tonight?"

"Not tonight, honey. I'm seeing Ginny."

"When are you going to drop her, Frank?" Althea's tone had changed to a whine. "I'm getting tired of sharing you."

"Baby, you know I need her for a while longer. I'm included in every function the governor has. I need the contacts—I'm not going to be a prosecuting attorney for the rest of my life. We've been over all this before."

"I know, but the time drags. How much longer?"

"I don't know." Frank's tone had sharpened. "If her father loses the election, I can drop her without a political setback as soon as he's out of office."

"Frank, that's a year away. I'm not sure I'll wait that long." Althea's pouting tone had reached the spot where Ginny was rooted to the floor.

"Come on, honey. We're so good together, you can't mean that," Frank had purred.

Virginia Gayle Johnson had shut her eyes and prayed for inner strength. A moment later she had knocked once, then pushed the door completely open and confronted them. Glancing from one to the other, she had noted the satisfaction on Althea's face and the near panic on Frank's.

With icy disdain she had informed Frank that she would not be seeing him anymore and then walked quickly out of the office. She had been angry and hurt, but the anger had been controlled and the hurt buried deep down, where it wouldn't show. She'd been well trained—smile in public, cry in private.

She had made it through the Christmas parties with other dates and treated the breakup with Frank as nothing major. However, her foundation had been rocked. It wasn't just losing Frank. In retrospect, she saw that he wasn't different from most politicians courting connections. He was an actor, always on stage, even in their relationship.

What really shook her was the thought that what she had achieved and who she had called friends were all directly related to the fact that she was the governor's daughter. What would happen if she were on her own? She had to find out, even for a short period of time.

She had talked to her father and arranged for time off. She wasn't sure how long. A few months at least, maybe longer. She knew she'd made the right decision in getting away from her past and starting fresh with time to sort out her life. She was expected to follow in her grandfather's and father's political footsteps, and in all honesty, she would like to do that. But right now she didn't want to be Governor Johnson's daughter first, and Virginia Gayle Johnson, her own person, second. She was an unknown in Arkansas, and she would make it on her own. Well, not quite on her own.

Ice crunched under the tires as Gayle pulled her car into the curb in front of Marta's shop. This was her fourth day in Arkansas, and she already had a job. Not bad for someone starting out fresh in life. "Lord, thank You for helping me start over," she murmured as she climbed the steps to the wide porch and pushed open the door to the first floor craft store.

Marta was at the work table, sewing an eye on a floppy-eared rabbit. She looked up as the bell above the door announced Gayle's entrance.

"How did it go, Gin? Do they need anyone?" Marta pelted her with questions.

"I'm not Gin anymore. I'm Gayle," she reminded her friend. "I have a job, and I start tomorrow morning." She recounted the interview with the history professor.

"No problem with the application?" Marta asked.

"None. The major qualification was the ability to type tests into a computer. I'll do a good job for them," Gayle assured her.

"There's no doubt about that. This is the university's lucky day." Marta finished her rabbit and carefully placed him in a box with five others. "Want some coffee?"

"Yes. I'm chilled to the bone. But stay put, I'll get it." Gayle walked to the back of the store and hung up her coat before pouring two cups of black coffee. She carried the fragile cups and matching saucers to the work table. "Marta, let me do that," she said as her friend strained to place the box of rabbits on the top shelf of the storage closet.

Gayle easily lifted the box of stuffed rabbits to the high spot and smiled down at her friend. In high school they had been called Mutt and Jeff because of their height difference.

The differences between the two women didn't stop there. Marta's long red hair was pulled back in a french braid, and her light complexioned skin never tanned. Gayle's dark brown hair was naturally curly and expertly layered so all she had to do was wash and comb it to look fashionably stylish. Her skin looked tan all year round, a trait inherited from her Italian great-grandmother.

In temperament and talent, they were equally miles apart, Gayle being sophisticated and academically inclined, while Marta was bubbly and artistic.

With all their differences, Gayle and Marta had remained friends even though distances separated them from the time of their high school graduation. Marta was the sister Gayle didn't have, and when Gayle needed a place to sort out her life, she immediately thought of Marta.

"Anything else go up here?" Gayle asked from the storage closet.

"No, that's it. Thanks," Marta said. "Gayle, remember the guy I pointed out to you yesterday at church?"

"Ted Novak?" she asked with a quick wink at her friend. It was a throwback to their communications system in high school. A wink meant a special guy.

Marta winked back. "Your memory of names boggles the mind."

Gayle smiled. "Part of my job—my former job," she amended. "So what about Ted Novak?"

"He called and asked me out to dinner tomorrow night." Marta's eyes glowed with excitement. "Would you like to go with us?"

"Not on your life. I don't believe a first date calls for a chaperone. Besides, I'll be exhausted after my first day on the job."

The bell above the door jangled, announcing a customer, and Marta scurried to the front of the store.

"I'll be upstairs," Gayle called to her friend and gingerly balanced her cup and saucer, winter coat, and purse as she climbed the curved staircase to Marta's living quarters. She sat at the kitchen table and spread out the newspaper at the want ads, circling apartments for rent. She couldn't continue to live with Marta, although her friend had made the offer. Of the original three upstairs bedrooms, one had been remodeled into a living room and another into a kitchen. Gayle had been sleeping on the couch.

Twenty-seven years old, and she had no place of her own. In school she had lived in a dorm and then in a furnished apartment, but with complete knowledge that it was temporary until graduation. By then her father was in the Governor's Mansion and had asked her to help him in Frankfort.

At first she had stayed in the big house with her folks, but soon she'd found a furnished apartment. Again, her living arrangement was a temporary measure. Only three years had remained of her father's term as governor, then she would be out of a job and need to move on.

She had always campaigned for him. Her mother disliked the spotlight, but Gayle had blossomed under it. From the time she was in first grade, she had been right beside her father, shaking hands, smiling for the cameras. By the time she was in high school, she had spent weekends traveling across the state giving speeches, attending luncheons and potluck dinners. Politics was a way of life for her.

After her graduation from Harvard, Gayle had been

courted by many prestigious law firms but had decided to work for her father simply because he had asked her. Her job had been an extension of the political life she had always known. As his assistant, she ran interference for him. Her dad had called her his chief of staff, and essentially that's what she had been, calling the shots that were not important enough to involve the governor.

Now her father was a lame-duck governor with not quite a year left in office. As the leading candidate in a field of six vying for his party's nomination for U.S. senator, he wouldn't need her help in the campaign until after he'd won the August primary. She'd give herself that much time to work out life on her own, then she'd return to work on his campaign. If he won, she wouldn't go with him to Washington but would look for a job with a legal firm or start her own practice.

For now, she needed a place to live. And again, a furnished place was a necessity. With Marta's purple pen, Gayle circled the few apartment ads that looked promising. Finding a nice place at the end of semester break in a college town might be difficult.

More than difficult, she decided after her fourth unsuccessful phone call. In desperation she looked up the phone book listing for a rental agency. She was surprised at the questions the agent asked and then at the phone call she received from the landlady. Gayle must have answered the inquiries correctly, for a half hour later, she was looking at a furnished, detached-garage apartment with Mrs. Connor, the owner of the main house.

Mrs. Connor was a little woman, around sixty, gray hair

pulled back in a bun, and smile lines around her mouth that told she was usually a jovial person.

"I didn't want to rent to college students, so I didn't put this in the paper. Matter of fact, I just decided yesterday to lease it. You just happened to be here at the right time."

That was the second time Gayle had heard that comment in just a few hours, and she felt God smiling down at her as she looked around the huge room. French doors on the west were the only means of entering the immaculate, one-room apartment, which was divided into living areas by large braided rugs. On one wall stood a fireplace with bookcases on each side. A couch, coffee table, and two easy chairs were grouped into a cozy sitting area that faced the fireplace.

A large round oak table and six chairs dominated one corner of the room, separated by a high bar from a modern kitchen that claimed the opposite corner. The final corner space held a four poster double bed, chest of drawers, and a rocking chair. An inconspicuous door between the kitchen and bedroom areas led into a dressing room with closets. Beyond that was the bathroom.

"I love it," Gayle said emphatically.

"I knew you would," Mrs. Connor said. "You seem the type. We fixed this place for my mother. All this furniture was hers." Her voice was tinged with sadness. "When would you like to move in?"

"This afternoon. I'm staying with a friend, so I'll pack up and haul my things over here. I start my new job tomorrow."

"Fine. Come to the house, and we'll get you a key and

sign the papers. I require a six months lease." Mrs. Connor was very businesslike now, much as she'd been when she'd questioned Gayle to determine her suitability as a tenant.

After signing the form, Gayle unloaded boxes from the trunk of her car. Marta had insisted she unload the back seat, mostly hanging clothes, when she had arrived. She'd have to go back to Marta's for those things.

Gayle had sorted through her household goods in Kentucky and had brought only what she considered essential. Boxes and boxes were stored at the Governor's Mansion. Mostly they were books, and she'd miss those, but she had packed what she could fit into her car.

The cold wind cut through her as she trudged back and forth from the car to the apartment. She unloaded the last box and sat down on the couch for a moment to look at her new home. It would do nicely.

She glanced at her watch. Quarter to four. She'd accomplished a great deal in one afternoon, but there was more to do before business offices closed at five. Although the boxes begged to be unpacked, Gayle made a list of errands at the bank, telephone office, and grocery store and then resolutely marched back to her car. In an hour and a half she had crossed off all the errands and had loaded her refrigerator with perishable items. She made it back to Marta's by five-thirty, quitting time.

"Do you have to move tonight?" Marta asked after Gayle told her about the new place.

"I start work at seven-thirty. You don't open your store until nine. I don't want to wake you up early when I know what a grouch you are first thing in the morning."

"You've got a point," Marta said and laughed. "Let's have a sandwich and then we'll start loading up."

As soon as they'd eaten a bite, the two women began carrying Gayle's belongings to their cars.

"No use in you bringing me home," Marta said. "Besides, we won't have to pack so tightly this way. Let's put the TV in my front seat," she said as they carried it between them from the back storage room to the car.

"What a great place!" Marta exclaimed the moment she saw the interior of the apartment.

The women braved the biting wind again and soon had the cars unloaded. Gayle found the coffeepot in a box and put on some coffee. The aroma filled the room as they unpacked boxes.

"First thing is to make the bed," Marta said. "That was one of my mom's moving rules. Then whenever you're tired, you can quit unpacking and hit the hay."

After an hour of labor Marta announced she had to run an errand. "By the time you get the bathroom stuff arranged, I'll be back," she said.

No sooner had she left than Mrs. Connor knocked on the door.

"How's it going, Gayle? I thought I'd pop over and tell you about the fireplace. It works great, and there's some firewood in the box here." She pulled out a large sliding drawer next to the fireplace. "You can fill this from the outside. We had it put in for Mom so she wouldn't have to go outside to get wood. There's still some wood out there, but you'll have to order more if you want to use this regularly. I'll give you the number, if you'd like."

"Thank you," Gayle said.

"I'll show you how to lay a fire up," Mrs. Connor volunteered. "There's a gas starter." She gave Gayle a step-by-step lesson, and soon a blazing fire added warmth to the apartment.

"A fire sure can cheer up a room," Mrs. Connor declared.

"It certainly can," Gayle agreed.

"Well, I'll be getting out of the way." She started for the door, then turned back. "Do you have any plants?"

"No," Gayle answered.

"Mom kept some hanging baskets around." She pointed to some hooks strategically placed around the large room. "My sun porch is loaded. If you want, I'll bring a few over tomorrow. Save me watering so many."

"I like plants," Gayle said. "Perhaps when I get home from work tomorrow we can move a couple."

"That'll be fine," Mrs. Connor said and smiled. "I'll see you then."

Gayle had finished with the bathroom and was placing books on the shelves when Marta returned with two white bags sporting her shop's logo and a bouquet of cut flowers.

"From the supermarket," she said, "but they'll brighten the place up." Like a magician pulling a rabbit from a hat, she unloaded the smaller bag. "You need something on the walls." She placed three framed lithographs on the kitchen table. "An Arkansas artist sells these in my shop, and she's quite good. I like this fall scene best."

"They're lovely," Gayle said. "I'll take them on loan

and return them to the shop when I move back to Kentucky."

"We'll see," Marta said. From the second bag she pulled a large quilted bedspread.

"Oh, no," Gayle said, recognizing the bedspread from the shop. It had hung on a quilt stand in the front window. "I can't use this, I might damage it."

"It's yours. A housewarming present, Ginny. I mean, Gayle. I can't tell you how much it means to me that you came to Arkansas to start a new life. You'll never regret this move."

Gayle glanced around at her new home, the cheery fire, the bright flowers, and her dearest friend.

"I know you're right. I already feel like a new person." Gayle hugged her friend. "Thank you for being here for me," she whispered. Silently she added, *And thank You, God, for giving me a friend like Marta.*

two

Dr. Landon J. Windsor studied the galley proofs spread out on his desk. Comparing printed quotes to his original manuscript required total concentration. He began to think the editor or printer didn't know the difference between the meaning of four dots at the end of a sentence and three. He marked another section.

The sharp tattoo of high heels in the hall distracted him. He'd come in quite early to work on the galleys. He could have stayed at home to read, but he liked his office and enjoyed talking with his colleagues when he took a break.

Last summer he had moved his office from the social science department, where he had shared office space, to the history department, where he could have a private office to write in. Because he taught one class in history, History of Political Parties, he qualified for the perk. It wasn't just the private office that had lured him to the history wing of the building. Dr. Dianne Steele, who taught sociology, had set her cap for him, and he wanted to avoid close contact with her.

At his last position at a college in Wyoming, he had learned to separate his professional and personal lives. Although he had been involved with Dr. Maryann Sellers, their relationship had lasted only seven months before he discovered that Maryann wasn't the woman he had thought she was. She had cleverly covered up her true nature. Her climb-over-anyone-on-the-road-to-success attitude alienated him, and he had broken off their relationship.

Unfortunately Maryann hadn't taken the breakup in stride. When Landon's first book had come out, she had wanted to share in that success. She had made life miserable for him, and when he had been offered the job at Arkansas, he had jumped at it. Although that had been three years before and his vision of Maryann had long ago faded, the lesson he had learned remained fresh in his mind.

The footsteps stopped outside his door, and he glanced up to see blue eyes he had seen before. A smile of recognition crossed her face, and he smiled in return. The woman from the parking lot. Who was she? What was she doing here? He had dreamed about her the night before after the single glimpse of her. Well, maybe two glimpses. He had turned back to see her again, and she had done the same thing. He took in her entire appearance, from her smart navy blue suit that spoke of quiet authority, to the short dark hair framing her oval face which revealed a softer feminine side.

Landon stood up behind his desk. "Hello," he said.

"Hello," she answered. She glanced above her at the shingle that jutted out into the hall. "Dr. Windsor?" At his nod, she offered her hand. "I'm Gayle Johnson." Her grip was warm and firm.

"I'm very glad to meet you, Miss Johnson." He put the emphasis on the "Miss" trying to ascertain if she was single or not.

"Single," she replied, holding up her left hand. "Mr. Windsor?" She emphasized the "Mr." with a grin.

He laughed out loud. "Am I that obvious?"

"Absolutely."

"And I thought I was being discreet." He motioned for her to sit down, and she took the chair he indicated.

She glanced at his desk. "Galley proofs, Dr. Windsor? Oh," she continued before he could answer, "Landon J. Windsor: *Trends in American Politics* and *The Chief Executive.* I should have recognized your name."

"Have you read them?" he asked, feeling pleased.

"Oh, yes," she replied quickly. "You're a very dramatic writer."

"Thank you," he said. Few people outside of the classroom read academic books. Who was this angel who had not only read his books but also liked his style of writing?

Gayle had skimmed his books only a month earlier, right after her break up with Frank. Her father had received a letter from Dr. Landon J. Windsor asking permission to follow the senate campaign and write about it. Not knowing his style or background, Gayle had done some research.

Her initial impression of Dr. Windsor's books, well written that they were, was that he showed all the warts, dwelling more on the negative than the positive side of personalities and issues. Because of the liberal bias she'd perceived, she had turned down his request to follow the governor's campaign.

Now that she thought about it, she couldn't remember telling her father about Dr. Windsor's letter. That last month in Kentucky was a blur in her mind and one she didn't want to dwell on. She turned her thoughts to the present.

"You obviously have a new book coming out," Gayle said. "What topic?"

"The civil rights movement in the sixties. No definite title yet—maybe you can think of something clever for me to suggest to my editor. We've changed it three times already."

"I can try, if you'll let me read it first." She'd like the opportunity to more carefully study his work, now that she'd met the author.

"That's an offer I can't pass up," Landon said. "You could catch the printing errors I miss."

He smiled across the desk at her, feeling an instant rapport. If he believed in love at first sight, he'd say he was in love. He felt bedazzled by the bright, witty, beautiful woman who had her entire attention focused on him. Was this how the prince had felt when he first saw Cinderella at the ball? His smile widened at his fanciful thought.

"I almost forgot why I came in. Do you have a key to the history office? I'm the new secretary."

Landon's smile froze, and his Cinderella fantasy evaporated abruptly. How could this happen? The girl of his dreams working in the same department?

"Yes, of course," he managed to reply in a rather distant voice. "Come with me, Miss Johnson, and I'll let you in. I'm surprised Dr. Webber didn't give you a key yesterday when he hired you."

She glanced curiously at him. His expressive eyes,

warm and friendly before, were cool. His words were clipped, a drastic change from his earlier manner.

"I talked with him after he interviewed you," he continued. "I should have surmised you were the new secretary," he said more to himself than to her. "He said you were a beauty."

"Thank you, I think," Gayle said. She stood to follow him. What had she said to make him look at her so strangely?

He walked her down the hall making sure there was a good three feet between them.

He was just unlocking the door when Dr. Webber stepped briskly into the building, letting in a blast of cold air with him. The professor took off his glasses, wiped off the fog the heat of the building had caused, and squinted at Gayle and Landon.

"Sorry I forgot to give you a key yesterday, but I thought I'd be in early enough to let you in. Guess you've met Dr. Windsor. He's actually in the political science department, but he teaches one class for us."

"I see," Gayle replied politely. She turned to Dr. Windsor, hiding the confusion she felt toward the younger man because of his strange mood swing.

"If you would like me to proof your book, just bring it to the office." She spoke in the business-like manner she thought would be expected of her.

"Thank you." Dr. Windsor did not commit himself about the galley proofs and walked away without so much as a good-bye.

Gayle turned her attention to Dr. Webber and asked

about the office routine and her general responsibilities.

Landon Windsor could hear her melodious voice as he marched back to his office. What an idiot he had made of himself! Flirting with a woman he didn't even know and then finding out she was an employee of the history department. He had vowed never to get involved with someone where he worked. *You never learn, do you, Windsor?* he chastised himself.

He plunked down in his chair and stared unseeingly at the long galleys on his desk. She'd read his books, and she'd volunteered to read these galleys. He should have known she was too good to be true. Looks like hers—with the carriage of a queen—that's what had piqued his interest yesterday when he'd first seen her. She walked as if she knew where she was going and no one was going to stop her. She had a determined air about her, and it must have been why he'd dreamed about her the night before.

In the history office, Gayle finished typing a syllabus for Dr. Sara Farrell, the only woman on the history faculty. She was gray-haired and about fifty, slightly built, but full of a vitality that reminded Gayle of Marta. Dr. Farrell shed some light on office routine, but Gayle learned more from the student worker, Annie Turner, when she came in at eleven-thirty.

"Sharon took early lunch hour," Annie explained, "while I watched the office."

"When do you eat?" Gayle asked the sophomore student. Annie wore her brown hair pulled back in a low pony tail, and her overly plump body was stuffed into tight faded jeans.

"Oh, don't worry," Annie said and laughed self-consciously. "I don't miss many meals. I eat at one-thirty. I only work two hours a day."

She gave Gayle directions to the Student Union Building where she could pick up a sandwich at the snack bar or eat a meal in the cafeteria.

As Gayle slipped into her coat, another professor came in, and Annie, a slight blush to her cheeks, introduced them. Dr. Swann was a young man, maybe thirty, with a head of curly blond hair, laughing eyes, a boyish grin, and a friendly manner that had Gayle grinning back.

"Going for lunch?" he asked. "I'm headed to the Union. Come on, I'll show you the way," he volunteered before she could answer. He winked at Annie, whose cheeks grew redder, and with a hand at Gayle's back, guided her out of the history building.

Gayle opted for the cafeteria, and lunch was good, despite rumors she'd heard about terrible college cafeteria food. The light-hearted chatter between herself and Richard Swann, soon on a first name basis, added to her enjoyment. They were dawdling over their coffee when Richard called out to Dr. Windsor as he passed their table. Gayle watched Dr. Windsor's smile for his colleague disappear as he noticed her. He nodded briefly to her when Richard introduced them.

"We've met," Gayle said distinctly.

"Oh?" Richard looked from one to the other. "Must have been quite a meeting," he joked. When neither of them laughed with him, he hurriedly asked Landon if their racquetball game was still on.

The two men spoke while Gayle sat excluded from the conversation. She contrasted Richard's boyish good looks in his casual sweater, khaki pants, and off-hand manner with the larger man standing only a foot away.

Dr. Windsor was tall with broad shoulders covered in a gray tweed sports coat that matched the color of his eyes. Those were his most outstanding characteristic, although the rest of his chiseled features would bear close scrutiny and pass a film director's idea of a masculine leading man. He dominated the area around them. Gayle was used to powerful men in powerful positions, but this one commanded respect in a fashion she couldn't quite define.

Why did he affect her so? She glanced up and found herself staring into those expressive eyes of his.

"What do you say, Gayle?" Richard was speaking to her.

"I'm sorry?" she said.

"How about having dinner after I demolish this guy on the court?" He inclined his head toward the towering man who probably had him by five or six inches and thirty pounds.

"Thanks, but I already have plans for the evening." She didn't explain that those plans were to carry plants from Mrs. Connor's house to her new apartment.

"Another time, maybe," Richard said.

Gayle merely smiled. She didn't think it was a good idea to see someone outside the office. It led to sticky situations. However, had it been the warm, friendly Landon Windsor she'd met first thing this morning, she would have made an exception. She didn't want to think about why.

"I'd better get back to the office," she said as she pushed back her chair. "Annie only works till one-thirty, and I have at least another ten questions for her. Please stay," she said to Richard as he started to get up. "You two can discuss racquetball strategy."

"No, I need to be getting back, too. You're going to have a busy day because I have three syllabi for you to type, and I hope to have the fourth one done soon. When enrollment starts tomorrow, this place will be hopping again. Coming with us, Landon?"

Landon had just walked into the Union for lunch, but he didn't hesitate before saying, "I was just on my way back when I saw you." Back to the snack bar was more like it, he admitted to himself, and wondered why he'd lied so easily to his friend.

He didn't join in the conversation on the brisk walk to the history building, but stayed on Gayle's right side like a silent sentinel. *What am I doing?* he asked himself. *Guarding her from Richard?*

When the trio arrived at the history building, he held the door for the other two, then quickly caught up so that he and Richard again sandwiched Gayle between them on the short walk to the office.

He caught the curious glances of Dr. Farrell and Dr. Webber from the end of the hall before he stepped aside to let Gayle enter the office ahead of him. Richard followed them in, whipped a folder out of Gayle's in basket, and proceeded to explain the pages he needed and the disk it should go on. Landon checked his empty mailbox, which he had checked only minutes before he walked to the Union. He waited until Richard had finished talking with Gayle and then followed his friend out of the office, starting an inane conversation about racquetball.

"What's wrong with you, Landon?" Richard asked as they walked down the hall toward their offices. "Don't you like her? She's quite a looker."

"Looks have nothing to do with her professional ability. We'll see how she does on your syllabi before I pass judgment on her as a secretary."

"Who's talking about her job?" Richard said and raised his eyebrows in a Groucho Marx imitation. "I'm talking about the woman herself."

"Don't you think that's inappropriate?" Landon said. He had never been one to advocate the false division between pompous professors and secretaries, believing it smacked of class distinction. However, he was adamant in his stand that professors shouldn't date staff members or other professors, for that matter. He and Richard had discussed office romances before, and he'd thought they had agreed on the subject.

"I've got work to do," Landon said before Richard could reply, and he ducked into his office. "I'll see you at the gym."

Richard stood in the doorway staring at him for a few moments before giving an irritating grin and raising his hand in good-bye.

"What am I doing, Lord?" Landon asked out loud. He now had nothing to eat for lunch and had probably alienated the new secretary. He'd wanted to talk to her, to smooth over his irritation that morning. On reflection he knew he'd been too abrupt in his behavior. He wanted a pleasant working relationship with her. After all, secretaries ran the place.

He didn't want to think of her as Gayle Johnson, for that conjured up images of dark hair, beautiful blue eyes, and lips that curled up in a natural smile. No, he would think of her as the secretary, and he didn't date anyone who worked with him. That was his policy, and it worked quite well.

His stomach growled. He reached in his pocket and pulled out two quarters, a dime, and three pennies. The basement vending machine would offer little for sixty-three cents, but he couldn't go into the office and ask Gayle, uh, the new secretary, for change for a dollar. He stood in the doorway of his office and made sure she wasn't in the hall before he slunk toward the stairs.

Gayle was thinking of Landon, too, as Annie bombarded her with questions.

"Do you always attract men like that?"

"That's just what I was going to ask," came Dr. Farrell's voice from the doorway, an amused smile playing on her lips. "Did you know those are the only two bachelors in the building?"

"It's not really what it seems," Gayle said and continued to sort through the new inter-office mail that had just been delivered. "Dr. Swann must be the department flirt and shouldn't be taken seriously, and Dr. Windsor, who's more of a distant person, just happened to be walking back when we were."

"I was going to caution you about those two," Dr. Farrell

said, "but I see I don't need to. See you later." She ducked back out the door.

"Well," Gayle said to her student worker to change the subject, "let's get to work. I'll tackle these." She motioned to Richard's folder. "And you start on Dr. Webber's."

"They always wait till the last minute to get stuff done," Annie informed her. "I have a friend who works in the duplicating department. She says they have to work overtime before each semester to get all the copies made."

"Then we'd better get these to duplicating today," Gayle said and inserted Richard's disk into her computer. She made some minor changes to the first syllabus on his disk and printed out a copy. The others were easily altered, too.

But at the end of the day, she was still working on the computer. Dr. Webber had a memo for all faculty members which he brought to her five minutes before closing. He handed her a key to the office at the same time. She didn't know if he was hinting that she should lock up after she completed the memo, but she decided to stay anyway and get it done. The printer was spewing out fifteen copies when Landon Windsor walked back into the office.

"Working late?" he said as he checked his mailbox again and instantly turned to leave.

"Wait," Gayle said.

Landon turned toward her, wondering what she could want. Would she accost him for his rude behavior today? It had taken all his courage to stop by the office on his way to meet Richard. He wanted another look at her and maybe the opportunity to apologize. But what could he say? *Sorry*

I snapped at you this morning. Sorry I ignored you at lunch. I really find you fascinating, and I don't want to.

"Here," she said and held out a sheet of paper she had just torn from the printer. "A memo from Dr. Webber. About enrollment."

Landon took the memo, his gaze steady on Gayle. He glanced down at the paper, then back.

"Thanks."

"Good luck on your game tonight."

"My game?"

"Your racquetball game with Richard," she said and nodded toward the sports bag he held.

"Oh, right. Thanks," he said and nodded briefly before turning and fleeing.

You are worse than an incoming freshman, he told himself as he walked toward the gym. *Infatuated over a woman's looks. I don't know a thing about her, except that she's single and she's read my books. Something doesn't ring true. A mystery surrounds Gayle Johnson. Why would a woman with her stately presence that screams authority and intelligence take a temporary job in the history office?*

As he marched into the gym, he vowed to find out.

three

Gayle ate a grilled cheese sandwich in front of the television news. She had kicked off her shoes as soon as she'd returned to her apartment, collapsed on the couch in front of the TV, and watched an ancient rerun of "Superman" before she could make herself change into jeans and begin her supper.

The news had been such a part of her life, it now seemed more like home to have the news anchor telling her of the events in Washington. After the national segment, Gayle was reminded of the distance between her former existence and her current one—she didn't know the names of the local politicians. At least she knew the name of Arkansas's governor. She had visited with him at a governor's conference just a few weeks earlier.

"Ah-ha," she said when she heard an announcement of a political party meeting Thursday night to nominate regional and state convention delegates. Here was her chance to learn more about the grass roots philosophy of politics without being personally involved. She made a note of the time and location. She'd have to consult her map of Fayetteville in order to find the place. Be easier to call Marta from work and get directions. She'd be glad when her phone was connected, for she felt isolated and out of touch.

She started at the knock on the door, but could see Mrs. Connor silhouetted against the french doors before she opened them.

"Here, let me take those," Gayle said and took two hanging airplane plants from her landlady. "These are gorgeous. Where do they get the best light?"

"Mom had them over by the east window," she said and pointed to the hooks. "I have a few more that might give this place a homey look."

"I'll walk back with you and carry them," Gayle said as she slipped on her coat.

In a few minutes they returned with three blooming African violets and a philodendron.

"They really do add a homey touch," Gayle said. "Thanks for letting me use them. Any special instructions?"

Mrs. Connor told her the watering schedule, then looked around at the apartment with a sigh.

"How long has your mother been gone?" Gayle asked softly.

"Five months. She lived here for three years before she got sick. I feel that if I turn around I should see her in the kitchen. Do you know what I mean?"

"Yes. When my grandmother died I had that same feeling every time I visited Grandpa. She should just be in the next room."

"That's it," Mrs. Connor said.

"Was your mother ill long?"

"Two weeks. She had a stroke. I didn't want her to linger like that, but I still miss her."

Gayle put her arm around Mrs. Connor. "She's singing with the angels now. That's what Grandpa always said when I'd cry about Grandma. Then I could imagine her up there leading the choir, just like at church. She was never one to be sitting on the sidelines, and I knew God would use her talents in heaven. How about your mom?"

Mrs. Connor stayed a half hour reminiscing about her mother. "I feel so much better now," she said. "George doesn't like me talking about Mom. I think he misses her as much as I do, but he can't stand to think about it. Men sure do react to things in odd ways. They think they are being straight and honest, but they hide emotions."

Gayle agreed, and as soon as her landlady left, she thought about Landon Windsor in that light and decided he was a typical man. She wasn't sure what emotion he felt toward her. When he had first met her, he'd looked at her with interest. She knew she wasn't imagining that. But the moment she had announced her position as secretary, a curtain had fallen over his expressive eyes and his distant manner had momentarily jolted her. Walking back from the Student Union, he had barely muttered two words.

Was it class consciousness that had altered his manner toward her? She smiled wryly. That would be a switch. In the past when she'd met snobs, her position in life had elevated her in their opinion, not lowered her.

But it didn't make sense that Dr. Landon J. Windsor would hold her job against her. She'd given that some thought during the day, and it didn't seem to fit with what she knew about him. But what did she really know? That he wrote books, that he taught school?

What do I ever really know about a person? she wondered. She had thought she was a good judge of character until she'd discovered Frank's true nature. From shortly before Christmas when she'd broken off with Frank until the end of last week, she had been surrounded by people. Now she was alone.

That's what she wanted, she told herself. Time to think about what she wanted to do with her life. Frank had not crossed her mind all day. Perhaps her feelings for him weren't as deep as she'd thought. Was he merely a person to fill her evenings, a suitable escort to take her to the political functions her job demanded? Had she used Frank as much as he'd used her? No, she decided. He was a dynamic aggressive district attorney, and she'd thought she'd loved him and had hoped there might be a future for them.

What had pushed Frank from her mind, or rather who had pushed him from her mind, was Dr. Landon J. Windsor. He had seemed so friendly and warm when she had first met him. She had felt an invisible connection between them.

She laid out her clothes for the next day, this time a pink wool suit with a silk blouse. She knew she would be more formally dressed than necessary, but her wardrobe revolved around her former job, administrative aide to the governor, and there was nothing she could do about that. She wasn't going to buy a temporary wardrobe for this job.

At work the next day, she hoped to understand more about Dr. Windsor. She knew he was there when she arrived. His office door was open, but she didn't walk down the hall to see him.

Gayle's day filled quickly as enrollment brought classes that closed too fast and classes that didn't make it and would be dropped if tomorrow's enrollees didn't fill them.

"We're going to have to add another section of American History 202," Dr. Webber told her. He decided on a time and room.

"Who'll teach it?" Gayle asked and grabbed a form, her pencil poised over the blank provided for the instructor.

"Just put staff," he said. "I'll have to do some shifting."

Gayle called it over to the old gym where lines had been formed by those who had failed to pre-enroll, and she posted the addition on the bulletin board.

While she stood in the hall, she overheard two coeds comparing their schedules and professors.

"Oh, don't take Dr. Talbott. He only touches reality occasionally and then it's by accident. Swann teaches that at ten, Monday, Wednesday, and Friday. See if you can change."

"I can't," the second coed answered. "I've got Windsor then for American Presidency, and you can bet I'm going to take it just so I can look at him."

"I've had him, and believe me, he's a hunk, but he doesn't give you a break for being female. Trust me, take Swann. . . ."

Gayle strained to hear more as the girls moved down the hall. It was the only mention she had heard of the two eligible bachelors that day.

During her lunch hour, she drove to Marta's shop and listened to a detailed account of her friend's dinner date.

"He sounds wonderful," Gayle said.

"He is wonderful," Marta said and extolled his fine points until Gayle had to leave for the university.

When she returned to the office, a syllabus for Dr. Windsor had appeared in her basket. Although Gayle typed it, had it duplicated, and put it in his mailbox, it had not been picked up when she left work that evening.

Tired as she was from the hectic day's activities, Gayle got out her city map and traced the route Marta had told her would get her to the community center. Resolutely she set out to learn more about local politics.

She arrived five minutes early at the community center and found a seat in the back of the large meeting room so she could leave early if the meeting went long. Glancing casually around at the various people, her gaze stopped suddenly when it rested on Dr. Windsor. Dressed in tan slacks, a darker brown corduroy sports coat with leather patches at the elbows, and a snowy white shirt with a brown club tie, he looked every inch the college professor. The leather-jacketed legal pad he carried added to the scholarly look.

Landon felt a stare, lifted his gaze from the small group around him, and felt his eyebrows arch in silent surprise. What was she doing at the meeting?

"Excuse me," he said to the two men and one woman with whom he'd been visiting. Against his better judgement, but with purposeful strides, he made his way to Gayle's side.

"Are you interested in Washington County politics, Miss Johnson?" he asked politely.

"Yes," she answered just as politely.

"I must admit, I'm surprised to see you here."

"And I'm surprised to see you here, Dr. Windsor. From reading your books, I assumed you belonged to the other party." Although she had given his books only a cursory reading, she'd been positive he was biased against her party.

"No, I'm registered with this party, but I don't work for either one, although I attend as many functions of both as I can. I listen and take notes, but I don't interact. I hoped I'd achieved a measure of balance in my books. Apparently, I failed." He smiled wryly.

The chairman banged on a table with his gavel and called the meeting to order.

"May I?" Landon asked and motioned toward the folding chair beside Gayle.

"Sure," she answered and watched him settle into the chair and open his legal pad.

"Are these notes for your next book?" she whispered.

"Yes," he whispered back. "I'm going to trace a political campaign from start to finish."

She nodded, well aware of the topic for his next book. She wondered if he'd found a candidate to follow on the campaign trail.

Gayle listened attentively to the discussion for a half hour, then found her mind drifting during a debate between two formidable old women over whether the party campaign headquarters should be located downtown or on highway 71. When someone moved the question be shelved until closer to June when the central committee could decide, Gayle stole a glance at Dr. Windsor. He caught her gaze, and she smiled and winked, sharing her amusement at the banal business of the party.

Landon couldn't believe she had winked at him. She looked as if she was surprised by it, too. That cute little wink was his undoing.

He leaned toward her and whispered, "Let's get out of here. It's about over anyway."

Gayle nodded her agreement. In unison they slipped out the back door into the foyer. Gayle reached for her coat from the rack, and Landon took it from her and held it while she slipped it on. He shrugged into his all-weather coat and asked, "How about a cup of coffee?"

"All right," Gayle said and smiled. A part of her mind told her she shouldn't go—that this man could somehow threaten her secret existence. But the Landon Windsor she had first met was back again, and she was fascinated by him.

They stepped into the crisp night, Dr. Windsor taking her elbow to steer her to the small cafe three doors down the street. Sitting in a booth facing each other, they ordered coffee.

"Well, what do you think?" Dr. Windsor said. "Should they rent a building on the highway or downtown?" he asked with mock seriousness.

"Those two old biddies do get carried away, don't they? Seems like there are always that type in political organizations, but they also do a great deal of the work."

"You sound as if you've experienced them before." It was a statement, but he was waiting for an answer.

"I've always been fascinated by politics, so I've gotten involved some at home." She certainly would not tell him she'd been raised as a political asset. Her father had been in politics as long as she could remember. She had met many politicians over the years, had known some very well, and still called the senior senator from Kentucky, Uncle John. No, she would not tell him lies, but she wouldn't tell him the whole truth either.

"And where is home?" Although it was the ritual exchange of first dates everywhere, he leaned forward as if her answer was of great importance.

"Here and there. I was an army brat the first few years of my life. I was born in California, but my father long ago retired from the service and now owns a cattle ranch in Kentucky." She failed to mention that her father wasn't there currently but was running the state government while her older brother ran the ranch outside of Bowling Green.

The waitress brought their coffee, and Dr. Windsor stirred a generous amount of sugar into his.

"Have you lived on the ranch most of your life? You seem to have more of a city girl quality than that." Was he seeing through her so easily?

"No, I've worked in different places. How about you?" she shifted the conversation away from herself. "Are you from Arkansas?"

"My family lives in Washington, but I've been in Arkansas three years, so it seems like home now. I like it here." Before she could think of another question, he asked, "Why did you come to Fayetteville?" His gaze searched her eyes. Gayle looked down at her coffee.

"I visited a friend here and decided I liked the area, too."
She hoped she sounded convincing.

"I think you're not telling all. As attractive as you are,
there must have been a man in the background somewhere.
Are you running away from someone?" He raised his
eyebrows as he asked the question, a habit she had noticed
before.

"I did just break up with someone, but I'm over it."

"A fiance?" he asked gruffly.

"Oh, no. Nothing that serious. I've never been engaged.
I just thought it would be nice to get into a different
environment for a while, away from family, and just start
over. All right?" she challenged. She hadn't meant to tell
him so much, but he'd drawn it out of her.

"End of conversation, you mean. All right, I won't ask
any more personal questions," he said lightly. He steered
the conversation back to the political meeting and that safe
subject carried them through the next few minutes. When
there was a lull in the conversation, Gayle asked about his
racquetball game.

"Was I right in assuming you usually beat Richard, Dr.
Windsor? Seems like your longer stride and reach would
be an asset."

"I think you'd better call me Landon," he said with
obvious resignation.

"When we're not at school," Gayle finished what she
thought he meant.

He smiled across at her. "Do I seem like a pompous
professor to you? Richard says I should mellow out, but I

like keeping my personal and professional lives apart. Makes things less complicated."

"Sounds to me like there's a woman in your background somewhere. Did you learn that lesson running away from someone?" she teased.

"Okay, you got me for saying that to you."

"A fiance?" Sensing that she was on to something important, Gayle wasn't about to drop the subject.

"No. It wasn't that serious. I've never been engaged," he imitated her.

She laughed. "So, did you beat Richard?"

"Yes. I usually do, but he gives me a good game. Do you play?"

"I love the game. Since I'm staff, can I reserve one of the university courts?"

"Sure. Do you have someone to play?"

"Not yet. Maybe I can find someone at the gym."

"I have a better idea. Why don't I take you on?" he challenged.

She stared into his eyes, knowing that he could easily beat her, but that this game was his way of seeing her again. But was he a threat? True, he had received a letter from her, but that was from Virginia G. Johnson of the governor's office. Surely he wouldn't make the connection. Her analytical mind also decided that his distant mood at school was his way of protecting himself against an office entanglement. Although she agreed that an office romance was not a good idea, she wanted to see him again. And it was only a racquetball game.

"Okay," she agreed.

"To make things interesting, let's say loser fixes dinner," he suggested.

So, she thought, he wants to go out on an actual date.

"Do you cook?" she asked.

"Would you believe Cordon Bleu?"

"No," she said and laughed.

"I didn't think you would. So, what do you say?" he asked again.

"I say, get out your apron, Landon."

four

They had talked another half hour before Landon had walked Gayle to her car. He didn't mention the racquetball game again, and she thought perhaps he had just been making conversation. But on Friday morning, he came into the history office and hung around until Dr. Talbott and Dr. Webber had checked their mail and departed, leaving the two of them alone.

"I reserved a court for us tomorrow morning at nine. Is that a good time for you?"

"Perfect."

"Good. Now about dinner. Since we're playing early, you'll have the rest of the day to cook a fabulous meal for me. Shall we say sevenish?"

"Seven is fine, but let's wait until tomorrow to see who's providing dinner. I'll meet you at the gym," she said and turned her attention to the student who had come in with a question.

Landon was in for a big surprise if he expected a gourmet meal from her. After talking with Marta on the phone that morning, Gayle had decided to take Landon to the church chili feed if she lost the game. Marta was in charge of publicity for the affair and had invited Ted Novak to attend the event with her.

Even though Gayle would like to know Landon better,

she was going to take this relationship, if it progressed that far without Landon falling back into his aloof professor persona, in a slow manner. Double dating with Marta sounded like an easy way to manage that. If they had fun at dinner, they would all go back to Gayle's to talk and relax in front of the fire.

Not that Gayle was going to give up the game without a fight, but she had a pretty good idea that Landon would come out ahead on the racquetball court.

By noon, Gayle was wishing for Saturday and the quiet time it would provide. The final day of registration was packed with student questions and long involved stories of why each one had to have this one class at this exact time. Although Gayle referred many students to Dr. Webber, she had to handle some of them herself. After Annie came in, she threw on her coat and headed to the old gym with the latest update on class closings.

"I'll drop this by for Dr. Talbott," she told Annie. "Then I'm having lunch and I expect you to solve all the rest of the problems for the day."

Annie laughed while solemnly promising to do just that.

Gayle stepped outside and inhaled the crisp air and absorbed the bright sunlight. She needed to be outdoors. At the State Capitol, she had scheduled herself regular coffee breaks and had used that time to walk around the block, getting away from problem solving and returning to her office with a fresh outlook.

Here she had no scheduled coffee breaks, but a coffee pot on the burner at all times. The professors dropped their change into a plastic cup marked "coffee money," and one of Gayle's duties was to keep the cabinet supplied with coffee and filters. Sharon must have made a trip to the grocery store shortly before having her baby, for the supply cabinet was full. At least that was one minor responsibility Gayle didn't have to worry about while she was learning her way around her new job.

Gayle watched the students mill about the campus as she strolled toward the old gym. On Monday, when the new semester began, they would walk with more purpose as they scurried from class to class. But today the sunshine had melted most of the snow, and the temperature was in the thirties. After that zero binge with its biting wind, the air felt like summer, inviting the students to amble from here to there.

As Gayle followed the sidewalk around the library, she dashed for the grass to avoid two men, one a cameraman walking backwards filming a group of men who were walking toward him.

The moment she recognized two of the men, she would have run except that they saw her at the same time.

"Ginny Johnson, what are you doing here?" David Stuart asked.

"Cut," called out the man beside the cameraman. He glared at Gayle.

Gayle remained silent. Usually quick on her feet, this time she was struck dumb. She had dined with David on several occasions in December at the special Southern Governors Conference. The chief aide for the governor of Arkansas walked up to her and took her arm, leading her back onto the sidewalk.

"Want to be in a news clip?"

"Oh, no," she protested quickly.

David turned to the governor. "Governor, you remember Virginia Johnson of Kentucky?"

"Of course, of course. How's your father?" the governor asked.

"He's fine, thank you. It's good to see you all. Sorry to have messed up your clip," she said to the cameraman and the man who was obviously the director.

"We're doing a promo for the university," David explained. "So, why are you in our great state, Ginny?"

"I came to see a friend and decided to extend the visit," she said and shifted her shoulder purse to hide the computer runs she held in her hand. "Your state is beautiful, Governor."

The Governor beamed. "You'll have to come back in the spring. We have flowering trees blooming everywhere."

"I'd like to," Gayle said, not explaining that she would be there in the spring as well. "I'd better let you get back to work."

"Can't you join us for lunch? We're about to break and take in some good ol' Arkansas barbecue."

"Thanks, but I'm meeting a friend," she said and smiled. Could she call Dr. Talbott a friend? she wondered. "How long will you be in town?"

"Flying out this afternoon."

The director cleared his throat.

Gayle extended her hand to the Governor in farewell. "Have a good flight," she said. She shook hands with David as well.

"It's always good to see you, Ginny. Will you be in Washington in April?"

"I'm not sure," Gayle hedged.

"Try to be there. I'll show you the sights of the city."

"Sounds like fun," Gayle said. "See you."

She turned to walk on down the sidewalk and saw Landon Windsor watching her from the steps of the library. Surely he couldn't have heard their conversation from that distance of maybe fifty yards. She waved to him as if she had nothing to hide and walked briskly on to the old gym.

Landon waved back and stared thoughtfully at the governor and a group of men who were being positioned by a man who was obviously directing a film.

Why was Gayle talking to them, and about what? He'd ask her when they played their game tomorrow. He was still amazed that he'd taken her for coffee last night and had asked to see her again. His "no dating someone from the office" rule had bitten the dust. And he didn't regret it. At least at this point. He'd see what tomorrow brought. Meanwhile, he wanted to do a little investigating into Gayle Johnson's background. Perhaps Dr. Webber would let him see her personnel file. With that purpose in mind, he headed back to the history building, forgetting why he had walked to the library.

Nine o'clock on a Saturday morning before the semester began was not prime time for the racquetball courts. Gayle knew the gym wouldn't be crowded, but she didn't expect the tomb-like atmosphere when she walked in.

Unfamiliar with the facilities, Gayle had opted for

wearing shorts under a jogging suit. She could shower and change at home instead of lugging street clothes with her.

A distant pounding drew her to the fourth court. She peeked in the window and saw Landon practicing. He wore white gym shorts and a red tee-shirt. On his right wrist was a sweat band and another circled his forehead. Gayle cautiously opened the door and slipped inside, all the while watching his style. He ran, swung, changed directions, ran, swung, with a distinct rhythm.

Landon knew she was there. He could actually feel her presence, but he continued to slam the ball against the far wall. *Am I showing off for her?* he asked himself and had to admit that he was.

He stopped the ball with his racket as it ricocheted back at him.

"Good morning," he said. "Are you ready for a little exercise?"

"Hi, Landon. Can I warm up before we start?"

He nodded and watched as she shed her winter coat then pulled off her jogging suit. She deposited her clothes in the corner by the door and picked up her racket.

"I hadn't noticed you were left-handed," he said. That really wasn't true. The other night he had noticed that she drank her coffee with her left hand, but he hadn't commented on it before, and at the moment he was tongue-tied and grasping for conversation.

"Could be an unfair advantage," Gayle said. "Got you worried?" she teased.

"Not yet. Let's see how you play."

Gayle dropped the ball and smashed it against the wall.

Landon stood to the side and let her hit the ball by herself for a few minutes before joining in. After a lengthy warm-up they started their game.

His greater strength was an asset, but she played with finesse, and their game was one of skill and adroit maneuvering, points won back and forth until the game ended in his favor twenty-one to eighteen.

"You're very good," Landon said after the last point.

Gayle leaned her racket against the wall and walked over to him, extending her hand.

"Good game, Landon."

He took her hand in his bigger one, casually draped his left arm around her shoulder, and dropped a quick kiss on her lips.

He hadn't intended to do that; it was as if he weren't in control of his actions. Instead of bells ringing and violins playing, he heard applause and catcalls.

He glanced up and saw an audience of five interested students watching through the glass partition at the top of the back wall. He recognized one as a former student of his. Well, what was done was done. With a grin, he lifted his arm in a victory wave.

"I believe your cover has been blown, Dr. Windsor," Gayle told him. "It appears there actually are some students who get up on Saturday morning." She had thought he had planned an early game knowing the gym would be deserted, and although it didn't appear to bother him that he'd been seen kissing her, no matter how innocent the peck had been, she wondered if that was truly what he was feeling.

"We'll see how fast their grapevine works." He kept his arm around her as he walked her over to her racket. "I predict it will be big news on Monday."

"Probably. About tonight, Landon. I think I'll take you out to eat instead of fixing dinner myself. Shall I pick you up around seven?"

"So you can't cook," he said. "I knew you were too good to be true."

Gayle laughed. "I can cook. And perhaps another time I will. But tonight I'll surprise you. Where do you live?" she asked as she slipped on her jogging suit.

"Why don't I pick you up?" Landon suggested.

"All right," she agreed. She told him her address.

"You live in Edith Wiley's apartment?"

Gayle shook her head. "I don't know Edith Wiley. Mrs. Connor is my landlady."

"Edith was her mother. I used to walk over for chess matches. We played two or three times a week. I still miss her."

"You walked over?"

"We're neighbors, Gayle. I live two houses past George and Eula Connor."

"Two houses?" she mused. "The two-story brick house, the one with the wide front porch?"

"That's the one. I'll give you a tour sometime," Landon said.

They walked out into the hall and Landon paused. "I changed in the locker room."

"Okay. I'll see you tonight."

"I'm looking forward to it," he said. "Next time we can play a couple of games, but this morning I need to review Monday's lessons."

"Maybe I should be playing Richard. Are we more the same speed?" Gayle asked.

"No, you're better, and I think you need to play someone who can beat you on occasion," he said adamantly. There was no way he wanted her playing with Richard. He might be his best friend, but he wouldn't trust him with Gayle. Besides, he had seen her first. He had also seen her with the governor. That thought popped unbidden into his mind, so he tackled it head on.

"I saw you speaking with our governor," he said, not posing it as a question, yet asking just the same.

"I was asked to be in the UA promo," Gayle answered.

"Sure," Landon said and nodded his understanding. "They sometimes use students to tag along in those films. I can see why they'd pick you."

"Thanks," Gayle said, thankful that she had glossed over that event so easily.

"Well, I'll see you tonight," he said and pushed open the door to the men's locker room.

Gayle drove home, tired, yet invigorated from her morning workout. She hoped she and Landon could begin to play on a regular basis. Racquetball at the club in Frankfort had been a part of her normal routine.

Gayle was about to step under the shower when she heard the phone ring. Her first phone call, and she had almost missed it.

"Marta," she exclaimed when she heard her friend's voice. "How was your date last night? Is he still wonderful?"

"Even better. We've seen each other three times now, and I feel like I'm on cloud nine. I'm in love, I'm in love."

"Seems to me you've been that way a few hundred times in the last ten years," Gayle said into the receiver.

"True. But those were all minor compared to this. Ted is a wonderful man. His computer business is going great guns, and he has more free time now that he's hired some other people to help out at his shop."

"More time to see you?"

"Exactly. He told me last night that he's seen me many times at church and wanted to ask me out, but he was too busy with the shop. It was one of the reasons he decided to take life slower. All work and no play, you know."

"I've heard that somewhere." Gayle twisted the cord around her index finger.

"What about your game?"

"I got beat. So, we'll meet you at the fellowship hall a little after seven."

"I didn't mean who won, I meant how was he?"

"He was good, and it was fun." For some reason, Gayle wasn't ready to confide about the little peck on the lips. For that's all it was, but she had felt tingles down to her fingertips.

"All right! I can't wait to meet him. This will be just like old times, Ginny. Double dating and all."

"Marta, you've got to call me Gayle. Be sure and don't

slip up tonight."

"Sorry. I'll be careful. I'm excited for you to meet Ted," Marta said. "He's different, special. You'll see."

"I'll reserve judgment until I meet him," Gayle said.

"Okay. But don't cross examine him."

"Marta, have I ever done that to your boyfriends?"

"Oh, please, Gayle," she emphasized the name. "Don't get me started."

Gayle chuckled and said good-bye. She and Marta had shared some great times. Marta's assorted boyfriends had stretched from high school dropouts to doctors and everything in between. She wasn't really unlucky in love, but she turned each potential beau into a good friend of the brother variety. Gayle hoped this time would be different.

By six-thirty Gayle was dressed and reading in front of the fire. Shortly before noon, the wood she'd ordered had been delivered, and she had taken off for the library and then carried a mystery with her to the laundromat. She was deep into the whodunit when the dryer had finished and had spent the rest of the day reading, taking time out to dress for her date in a gray silk blouse and a darker gray wool skirt.

With only ten pages to go, the detective had gathered the suspects in one room and was about to announce the murderer. The knock outside interrupted her at a crucial moment, but as soon as she'd opened the door to Landon, the plot of the book escaped her mind.

Under his opened overcoat he wore tan slacks and a burgundy sweater with a white collar peeking out. He stood by the door, hands in his pockets, dwarfing the room, and looked around with interest.

"I haven't been here since Edith died. Almost the same furnishings, but missing all her little knickknacks, the doilies she had on every little table." He turned to Gayle. "She'd be glad you're living in her home. You fit here, and you look lovely tonight," he said, his eyes showing his appreciation.

Gayle smiled at him. "Thanks. Ready to go have a deluxe meal?"

"Sure. Now, where is it we're going?"

"A surprise for a few more minutes. Actually we're going to meet some other people."

"Your friend that drew you to Arkansas?"

"Yes. Marta Hanks and her friend Ted Novak. Marta's a bubbly, creative person. You'll like her. I haven't met Ted, but I know he owns a computer store." Gayle reached for her coat off the hall tree, and Landon took it and helped her with it.

She still didn't tell him where they were going, but gave him block by block directions to the fellowship hall.

"We're going to church?" he asked as he parked the car in the lot.

"Is that all right?" She searched his face for a reaction. "It's a chili supper. Marta's on the planning committee."

"That's fine. I had envisioned the winner of our game getting something a little more exotic than chili, but it happens to be one of my favorite foods."

He took her arm and ushered her to the basement door.

"Have you been here before?" she asked.

"Not for church. This hall is used by civic groups. The Kiwanis hold their pancake feed here."

"Where do you go to church?" Gayle asked. She had wondered about his spiritual life, but they hadn't discussed it.

"There's a little campus church a couple blocks east of Old Main. A friend of mine is the minister. It's not fancy, but it gives the students without cars a place they can walk to easily. It's more of a gym type. . .well, it's hard to describe the atmosphere. Would you like to see it?"

"Yes, I would," she said, feeling relief that Landon was a Christian. "Church has always been a part of my life, and I'd like to find a church family here." In the crowd ahead of her she spotted Marta's red hair. "Follow me," she said and took Landon's hand.

After introductions were made, Gayle watched the interaction between Marta and Ted as they made their way through the line. Ted stood a good head taller than Marta, but his body language, leaning toward her, listening intently to what she said, told Gayle that he just might be different than the rest of Marta's suitors. The others had needed a shoulder to rely on, and Marta had fallen into the mothering trap. This man didn't want a sister or a mother, and his shoulders were broad enough to handle his responsibilities and hold a woman who might need comfort, too.

As they took their seats at long tables set up for the occasion, Gayle glanced across at Marta and gave her a slight nod.

Marta beamed. "I told you," she said.

"What's that?" Ted asked.

"Crackers?" Marta smiled sweetly and picked up the basket and handed it to him.

five

"Shall we go to your apartment, Gayle?" Marta asked. "I have my new game in the car."

The two women had exchanged secretive looks and quick winks throughout the meal. And that had included two bowls of chili for the men, plus a piece of pie for dessert. By the time the last crumb had been eaten, Gayle knew that Marta approved of Landon, and she had conveyed her opinion of Ted to Marta. The communications system they had employed in high school still worked.

"What game?" Landon asked.

"I have one of the first special anniversary editions of Trivial Pursuit to hit Fayetteville," Marta announced. "Are you game? Maybe women versus the men?"

"I think Landon and I can manage that," Ted said.

"This will be a piece of cake," Landon bragged when the foursome were sitting at the round table in Gayle's apartment. He and Ted set up the board and distributed the game pieces while Gayle made coffee.

"Let the games begin," Marta said when she had carried the last cup to the table.

Conversation flowed with good-natured teasing while the two teams battled back and forth, answering questions that ranged from foreign policy to science to show business rumors. The teams were evenly matched. The game came down to one question. And the men won.

"I can't believe it," Marta said. "We do this so well."

"It was the luck of the draw," Gayle said. "They could have easily gotten our question and they wouldn't have known the answer either. Well, good game." She shook hands with Ted and then held out her hand to Landon.

"This is it? A handshake for winning? I think you can do better than that," Landon said with a grin.

"Yeah," Ted seconded. "I think we should be rewarded."

"Would another cup of coffee do?" Gayle offered.

"No way," Ted said. "Are you ready to go?" he said to Marta. "I think this is one conversation we'll complete on our own."

As soon as they left, Landon pulled Gayle into his arms and kissed her soundly on the lips.

"Now that's how you're supposed to congratulate a winner," he said. "Want to try it?"

"I think I can handle that," Gayle said and drew his head down to hers. She liked kissing Landon. She liked it a lot.

"That's more like it," Landon said after she had pulled away. "Now that you know how to reward a winner, want to try another game?"

"I don't think so," Gayle said and laughed. "I will put on another pot of coffee if you'd like."

She cleaned up the kitchen while Landon stacked the question cards and put the game pieces in their storage bag.

"Gayle, here's another question for you. Who wrote *A Study of History*?"

Gayle paused at the sink where she was filling the coffee

pot. "Let's see," she said and thought a moment. "Arnold Toynbee. He believed the growth of civilization was a spiritual process and historical decline was the result of spiritual failure. What did he end up with—twelve volumes?"

She turned to find Landon looking at her oddly. He'd already put the game away.

"Where did you go to school, Gayle?"

"School?" She had trapped herself.

"School," he repeated. "As in reading, writing, and arithmetic."

"Bowling Green High School. Marta and I were classmates there," she stated as calmly as she could. Where was all this leading?

"You're very good at trivia. I'd go so far as to say excellent. You're either the best-read high school graduate I've ever met or you've had college training. And everything about you—your demeanor, your sophistication, your self-assurance—tells me you've been to college."

Gayle had vowed not to lie to Landon, but how could she pass over this matter without making a big deal of it?

In her best Boston accent she said, "I attended Harvard, of course."

"Of course," Landon said imitating her accent. "With your interest in politics, why not Harvard Law School?"

"All right," Gayle said with a forced laugh. "I'm a graduate of Harvard Law School."

"So you're not going to tell me. Why are you being so mysterious? I'd like to know you better, Gayle, but you're not being truthful with me." He took hold of her shoulders and his gaze searched her eyes. He lowered his arms and straightened to his full height.

"You did graduate from Harvard Law School, didn't you?"

"Magna Cum Laude," Gayle said in her normal voice.

"You're a lawyer?"

"Yes. I passed the bar."

He knew she hadn't put that on her job application. Although Dr. Webber had not shown him the form when he'd asked, the professor had told him what he knew about Gayle's background.

"Then why are you masquerading as a secretary?"

Gayle took a deep breath. "Landon, I want you to trust me. Trust me enough not to ask questions. I won't lie to you. I may not have told you everything, but what I have told you is the truth. Remember the other night, I told you I came to Arkansas to have some time to myself? My job here is only temporary, so I won't hurt my employer by walking out on him when I need to go home again. But I don't want to talk about it, not now anyway." She shook her head, as if that would dislodge a bad memory.

"He hurt you that badly," Landon muttered.

"Who hurt me?"

"That man you're running away from."

"No, he didn't. He just made me see some things I was blind to before." She smiled at him, trying to lighten the situation. "Landon, I'm not a criminal, nor do I have a past I might be ashamed of."

"I never thought that."

"Good. Now, can we be friends, with no questions asked?" She looked beseechingly up at him.

"All right, at least for now. When you're ready to confide in me, I'll be here."

"I appreciate that. Now, do you want another cup?" She turned back to the coffee pot to measure out coffee.

"I think I'll pass, thank you." He took the coffee scoop from her and placed it back in the coffee can.

"What I would like is to hold you like this." He pulled her into his arms and guided her head to rest on his chest. He held her for the longest time and Gayle felt as if she had come home. She wanted him to hold her for always.

"Would you go to the campus church with me tomorrow? We could pick up something to eat afterwards."

"I'd like that," Gayle said.

"I'll pick you up at ten-thirty." He tilted her head up and kissed her, then slipped an arm around her waist and walked with her to the door.

"Good night," he said. "I'll see you tomorrow."

After he left, Gayle poured water out of the coffee pot and put the trivia game on the bookshelf. Marta must be in love, she mused, to have forgotten to take her game with her.

And what about me? she thought as she got ready for bed. In love? Hardly. She had just met Landon, she wasn't about to fall in love with him after knowing him a total of four days. But there was something special about the man.

Gayle turned off the light and crawled into bed. Her night time habit of talking to God had always helped her sleep peacefully. Tonight was no exception.

"Dear God, thank You for today and thank You for my new friends. Please, God, show me the way with Landon. Don't let me make the same mistake again. And please understand that I'm not lying to him. I'll tell him about my family when the time is right. I really need to know that he likes me for me and not for what he will gain from it. Please help me, Lord."

Gayle was unprepared for the appearance of the campus church the next morning when Landon drove them into the parking lot. White paint that was beginning to peal on the exterior made her think the interior would be in the same sad condition.

The inside was one large room, a half basketball court. The walls were freshly painted a soft tan color with bright yellow drapes at four high windows. Folding chairs, ten in a row, covered the hardwood floor.

Although there were a few children with their parents, most of the members appeared to be students who milled around or talked in small groups. Dressed in everything from jeans to dresses and suits, they sat down en masse once a young man of thirty-something walked to the front of the room.

"That's Clark Rossiter. He teaches in the civil engineering department, but he's also an ordained minister. He runs this church," Landon whispered to Gayle once they had taken seats in the middle of a row.

"Let's meet our neighbors," the minister said and stepped to the front row to shake hands with some of the students.

Gayle introduced herself to the girl sitting beside her

and then shook hands with the young men behind her. Landon introduced her to a professor on his left.

"Do you know the members?" Gayle asked.

"Most of them. I've had a few of the students in class, but the majority of them are from the engineering school—that's how they know Clark—and they don't take much political science."

Clark Rossiter returned to the front of the large room and led the gathering in the Lord's Prayer. "Let's enjoy a number by Southern Hospitality."

Three young men walked to the front. One carried a guitar, another a violin, and the third stepped behind a keyboard that sat on a small table.

With the drum beat vibrating from the keyboard, the trio played an upbeat song that Gayle didn't recognize. They followed it by leading the group in singing "Rock of Ages." Gayle hadn't heard that song since she'd watched a rerun of "Little House on the Prairie" and certainly never from such an odd trio. She stole a glance at Landon, who was singing in a strong baritone voice.

Clark Rossiter stood behind a music stand and talked about the power of prayer. He read a poem and a Bible verse and asked for discussion. A couple students stood and told how prayer had helped them through a crisis.

"I don't think this is verbatim, but I think of Psalm 18 when I'm in need," one young man said. "'He reached down from on high and took hold of me; he drew me out of deep waters. . .in the day of my disaster. . . .the Lord was my support. He brought me out into a spacious place; he rescued me because he delighted in me.'"

After he sat down, the congregation sang another song, the minister asked a blessing, and the group dismissed. Landon and Gayle hung back, waiting for the students to file out ahead of them.

"There are bathrooms back here and an office of sorts. This kitchen sees lots of use since the dorms have no food service on Sunday nights," Landon said as he walked Gayle around the area.

"Landon." Clark had walked up behind them. "You've brought a new recruit."

Landon made introductions and Gayle shook hands with Clark Rossiter. He was small for a man, no taller than Gayle, and his grip was firm and his eyes twinkled with inner happiness.

"I enjoyed your...talk this morning, Reverend Rossiter," Gayle said.

"Thanks. And call me Clark. I'm sure you noticed we're very relaxed here. No big organ or ladies circle or even a church bulletin for the service. We don't have a big budget. A lot of the students don't have much money. Many have part time jobs or are on scholarships. But they work around here and come spring, we have a big crew lined up to paint the outside. Perhaps you'll join us."

"Have you ever painted, Gayle?" Landon asked.

"The only paint brush I've ever held was in art class, and I was no Michelangelo," Gayle admitted with a laugh.

"She might be better off carrying cold drinks to the workers," Landon teased. He rested an arm on her shoulder and ushered her toward the front door.

"I'm glad you came, Gayle," Clark said. "Most of our

students are dedicated to the Lord and have home churches, so we have a very loose structure here," he said. "We concentrate on the Golden Rule and stress that God is love and worship Him. We're within walking distance of the dorms, and we provide a place where students can come worship, have clean fun with others, and play a little basketball. Landon's on one of our teams."

They had reached the door. On a small table beside it stood a collection basket with change and a few bills. Landon reached in his pocket and dropped in a large bill. Gayle pulled some money from her purse and placed it in the basket.

Landon opened the door and they stared at the rain that had started since they had entered the church. "Stay here, Gayle, and I'll pull the car around," he said and dashed outside.

"Landon is a fine Christian man," Clark said. "Have you known him long?"

"No. But I admire all I know about him so far."

"He helps with the kids here. And he keeps the refrigerator well stocked with soda pop. Says they all need a cold drink after a game. We couldn't do without him. He's a good role model for the students."

Landon drove up in front of the church, and Gayle ran down the steps to the car. As soon as she was inside, she waved to Clark.

"He seems very nice," she told Landon.

"He's terrific with the students. He's not paid for ministering to them, and he gives a great deal of his time. He says it's his calling, and engineering is his vocation."

Landon turned on highway 71 and drove north. "Have you been to the AQ Chicken House yet? It's an Arkansas institution."

"I've missed it, but chicken sounds good."

It was delicious. But dinner was over all too soon. Landon gave Gayle a tour of Fayetteville, but the rain and the cold shrouded the landscape in gray.

When Landon took her home, he declined her offer of coffee. "I'd like to finish those galley proofs this evening. If you're still willing to read them, I'll bring them over tomorrow evening."

"I'd love to read them," Gayle assured him. "Thank you for dinner and taking me to church today. I'd like to go again."

He smiled and kissed her before leaving her at her door.

That kiss was still on her mind when Annie came into the office the next day. Work had been hectic with the first day of classes and students coming by dropping and adding classes, yet Landon stayed in the forefront of Gayle's mind.

"Anything newsworthy here at the office?" Annie asked with a sly smile on her lips. "Or out of the office, for that matter?"

"Okay, Annie. Say what you have to say," Gayle conceded.

Annie sat down in the chair facing Gayle's desk. "I'd just like to know how you did it. Going out with Dr. Windsor is a major accomplishment."

"Not so major, Annie. We just played racquetball, a friendly game, that's all," Gayle pointed out.

"My sorority sister saw it and she said it was a bit more than a friendly game."

"Who's playing friendly games?" Richard Swann said from the doorway. "Can I play?"

"Gayle and Dr. Windsor played racquetball Saturday morning," Annie volunteered before Gayle could give her a sign to be quiet. Landon had made it clear that he wanted his professional and personal lives separate.

"No kidding? Landon broke down and took someone out from the university? I've got to hand it to you, Gayle. That's a first. He dates quite a bit, but never anyone from here. It's his cardinal rule."

"We played racquetball. I wouldn't call that a date." Gayle didn't mention the chili supper, church, and Sunday dinner.

"Did you beat him?" Richard asked.

Gayle grinned. "No, but I gave him a good game. Eighteen to twenty-one."

"Not bad. Hey, would you like to play me? I'm not quite Landon's speed, although I've beaten him a couple times," he mentioned proudly.

Gayle hesitated. Landon had told her not to play Richard, but she didn't see what it could hurt. He was probably more on her playing level. Besides, according to Richard, Landon went out a lot. That bothered her, although it didn't surprise her. A man didn't learn to kiss like he'd kissed her by kissing his sister on the cheek.

"Sure, I'll play you. When?"

"I'll get a court," he said, moving to the phone.

While he called, Gayle lined out work for Annie. She

glanced at her watch. Her lunch hour was slipping away.

"I'm on hold," Richard announced. "Hey, Landon. I hear you played racquetball with Gayle," Richard said, then turned back to speak into the phone.

Gayle was aware of Landon's presence the moment he walked into the office.

"Can't get a court today, but we've got one for tomorrow at five," Richard told Gayle.

"Fine. I'll meet you at the gym," Gayle said.

"You don't mind if I cut into your time, do you, old friend?" Richard patted Landon on the back.

Landon smiled although he was not pleased, and he didn't answer the question. "I'll come watch the game," he said instead. "She's good. You'll have your work cut out for you." He turned his attention to Gayle. "I finished the galleys after I took you home yesterday."

"I'll be glad to read them, Dr. Windsor."

"Oh, I think you can call me Landon at school, too."

Gayle stared at him. What was he doing? He'd made a point of not mixing his professional and social lives, and yet here he was announcing he was dating her.

"Why don't you come over for dinner around six-thirty?" he asked. "I'll give you the galleys and that tour I promised."

six

Gayle switched on a light as soon as she entered her apartment. She was home before five, but dusk was already settling in the winter sky. She glanced over at the cold hearth wishing for a cheery fire to warm her hands. Another front had passed through in the afternoon, and the thermometer had dipped twenty degrees in less than four hours.

"And Marta says this is not typical Arkansas weather," she grumbled as she laid logs on the andirons and lit the gas starter. She quickly changed her herringbone suit for a pair of jeans and a red wool sweater, then made herself a cup of hot chocolate and sat on the rug in front of the fire, staring into the flames.

"What am I doing here, Lord?" she asked. "Am I running away from one crisis and finding the same thing here?" As was her custom when confronted with a difficult issue, she turned to God for direction.

She thought about Landon. Now he knew her profession. Was that a problem? It shouldn't be. She may have been admitted to Harvard because her father and grandfather were alumni, but she had made it on her own there and graduated with high honors. She could have had a job with a prestigious law firm, but had decided to work for her father simply because he had asked her. Funny, she had always thought of herself as an independent person, but she had always taken the easy road and done what her father suggested.

Perhaps that was because they were interested in the same things. Law fascinated her and the political scene was so exciting. She liked the feeling of power it gave her to have an influential position in the government, and she liked knowing the dynamic people with whom she was constantly associated.

"Is that wrong, God? I've not misused power, misdirected it, or used it to hurt someone," she defended herself.

When did disillusionment claim her? Was it really Frank who had made her see that she'd been used? When she'd first met him, she'd been so impressed with his positive charisma, his innate charm, and his ambition. He had flirted with her before they had discussed occupations or backgrounds, although, she decided now, he must have known of her family connections. Back then, she had thought he was interested because she was attractive. Plenty of men had told her so, and she could see that in her own mirror. She wasn't conceited about her looks, just thanked God that He had blessed her with a combination of looks and brains.

So where did things go wrong with Frank? Had she failed him when she had continually rejected his physical overtures? Although that theme had haunted her before, she couldn't accept it. She had never felt a strong physical chemistry between them that might cause her to toss aside her beliefs and upbringing. She had felt more desire for Landon than she had ever had for Frank, and she'd only known Landon a week. But she felt safe with Landon. He wouldn't ask her to forsake her beliefs because, she instinctively knew, he shared them.

She stared into the fire. Was she here to escape one relationship just to replace it with another? And where was this relationship going, she'd like to know.

"Please help me, God," she whispered.

A sudden knock on the door startled her out of her reverie. "Come in," she called without getting to her feet and watched as Landon strolled in and quickly shut out the frigid air.

"You shouldn't invite someone in without knowing who it is," he chastised her. "Please be more careful in the future."

"Okay," she agreed. "Am I late? Is it six-thirty already?"

"Not quite. I thought I'd walk you over since it's so dark out." He walked over to the fire and held out his hands. "Feels good."

Gayle climbed to her feet, collected her purse, and put on her coat while Landon banked the fire and shut the fireplace doors.

Landon led her out into the cold night and onto the sidewalk in front of the Connors' house.

"The Phillips live here," he told her and motioned to a second stately home they passed. "And the next one is mine. I had it built two years ago."

They climbed the steps that led to his front door. Gayle appreciated the beauty of the large entry hall. As Landon took her coat, she examined the room. A walnut staircase led to the second floor, burgundy drapes covered the west window with an antique love seat under it, and a high ceiling held a candle flame chandelier. A brass hall tree stood to the left of the front door and an arched doorway led into a living room.

"I'm really surprised, Landon. I expected a modern home since you had it built."

"I like the style of older homes, but not the problems one inherits with age. So I asked the architect, Alex Benton from the School of Architecture, for a new home with all the modern luxuries, but in a period house. And this is what I got." He waved his hand around.

"It's lovely."

"I'll give you the tour after dinner." He ushered her toward the back of the house and into the kitchen. "Have a seat." He pulled out a chair for her at the kitchen table, which sat at one end of a long kitchen in front of a fireplace, then he opened the oven and extracted bread sticks.

Gayle sat quietly watching Landon's activity at the other end of the kitchen which held cabinets in a U shape with a center work space. Her gaze wandered through another wide arched doorway to a formal dining room. She was glad they were eating in this wonderful, old fashioned-modern kitchen. The fire in the fireplace gave a cozy glow to the room.

Landon placed steaming bowls of stew on the table, followed by the bread sticks.

"This smells wonderful," Gayle said.

Landon grinned. "It's from a can, but I add my secret spices to give it some zip."

Gayle buttered a bread stick and took a bite of the stew.

"Is garlic one of your secret ingredients?"

"How'd you know?"

"Lucky guess," she said and wondered if he had added two cloves to one small can of stew.

After dinner, Landon escorted her back toward the front of the house and through another door she hadn't noticed earlier that led to his study.

It was definitely a man's room. The walls were lined with bookcases, but weren't crammed with books. The hard bound volumes were artfully arranged with pictures and wooden models of boats, kerosene lamps, and other masculine type bric-a-brac. A rectangular table sat at one end with two cane-bottomed chairs on each side. Landon moved a thick bundle of galley proofs from the desk to the table. He extracted two pens from a tall, lidless ceramic jar on a bookcase and handed one to Gayle.

"Interesting pencil holder," Gayle commented as she took a seat at the table.

"My niece made it for me for Christmas last year," he replied as he sat down beside her.

"Do you have many?"

"Pencil holders?"

"No, nieces."

"Nine," he said and smiled. "And twelve nephews."

"That's quite a family. How many siblings do you have?"

"Five brothers and two sisters. What about you, or is that a legal question?"

"I have one brother. He's three years older than I. Where do you fit in chronologically?"

"I'm the fifth one. Morgan, Marshall, Cathy, Bill, Landon, Michael, Cecil, and Melba," he rattled off. "And, yes, I'm the only single one."

She laughed. "Now how did you know I was going to ask that?"

"I could see your logical mind trying to fit twenty-one kids with their parents. We believe in large families."

"I see. My brother Stan is married and has two children."

"What? Volunteering information about your background? Before you know it you'll be telling me your deep, dark secret," he teased.

"Very funny," she answered sarcastically. "I was just carrying on my end of the conversation."

"Admit it, Gayle. You're interested in my background because you're interested in me. A person's childhood has a lot to do with who they become as an adult, and by knowing my past, you'll know me better. I feel the same way, but you won't let me ask questions." The frown on his forehead told her that he was serious.

"I would like you to know me better, Gayle, and then perhaps you'll trust me. What do you want to know?"

Gayle pursed her lips in thought. "Where did you get the money to build a house like this?" She thought that would stop him because most people didn't like revealing their finances.

He answered without pausing. "My ancestors helped settle Seattle, Washington, and the family still has major landholdings there. Not just on the outskirts, but in downtown Seattle. My father set up a trust so that each of his children, on his or her twenty-first birthday, inherited stock in the family real estate corporation.

"I attend a yearly meeting of the stockholders, which is actually a large family reunion—complete with grandparents, aunts, cousins—and receive my share of the dividends. We own two hotels, several office buildings, apartment complexes, etc. I've invested my money wisely over the years, and it continues to earn more. Of course my salary here at the university and royalties from the books help, too."

"That's quite impressive."

"I'm only out to inform."

"Yes, well, you won't be getting any royalties if we don't get to work on these proofs. Tell me what you want me to do." Gayle had enough to think about. She needed an impersonal topic.

"It's a little late for rewriting, although there are portions I've found that could use it. We're after typographical errors. I've found some, but I'm sure you'll find more. I tend to skim over sections and miss the errors. Simple enough?"

"I think I can manage, but I'd do it much faster and could concentrate better if I were alone. May I take these with me? I promise I'll guard them with my life." With him sitting next to her, Gayle was doing well just to breathe.

"No need to carry it that far. There are other sets. Mark in the margin like this." He showed her an error he had noted. "Do you think you could have them finished by Friday? I need to get them back to my editor."

"That shouldn't be a problem." She glanced at her watch as she rose from the chair. "I can read for a couple hours tonight."

Landon emptied some papers from a large bulky envelope onto his desk. "My graduate assistant is doing a lot of the footwork for my next book," he said and folded the galleys and stuffed them into the now empty envelope. He handed it to Gayle, who was staring at the papers he'd dumped on his desk.

"Looks like a mess, doesn't it? We've sent questionnaires out to candidates across the country. I'd like to follow a campaign for the U.S. Senate. A federal position would create a wider reading public than a race for a state house."

Gayle stared down at the top sheet, a letterhead featuring the seal of the state of Kentucky with her signature at the bottom. "Virginia G. Johnson, Assistant to the Governor."

With shaking fingers she reached out and picked up the pile, shuffling through them and putting her letter on the bottom.

"Oklahoma would be an interesting state," she said in a voice she hoped sounded normal. "No incumbent and four candidates running in each party. Why haven't you already chosen a candidate? Then you could follow him or her through the primary as well."

"In a sense, I will. I'm on sabbatical in the fall, and I'm not teaching summer school. So from May tenth until after the November election, I'll be on the campaign trail. But I need a candidate who will win the primary. Some of the races are too close to call, and I wouldn't want to follow a loser through the primary, then have to pick another candidate."

Gayle looked through a few more questionnaires. "Did your graduate assistant send these out?" she asked. Inside she was quaking. Did he already know who she was?

"Yes," Landon said, warming up to his subject. He leaned against the desk. "I'm teaching Tom Lancing practical research skills. He's listed the thirty-three Senate races, discovered who has filed in each party, which races have incumbents, and sent each candidate a questionnaire. Gayle, are you interested in this?"

"Oh, you know I like politics. Power struggles and the challenge of a race," she said.

"That's what I like, too. I hope to present such a clear picture of a campaign that the readers will feel as if they're backstage with the candidate, making decisions, facing the press, and trying to convince the voters."

"I'm sure you'll do a fine job."

"Gayle, would you like to help with the selection process? You might have some insights that could make a difference."

"That would be very interesting," she said and felt she'd never uttered a truer statement. Perhaps she could steer him away from the Kentucky questionnaire. "Have you had any positive replies?"

"Some. And some definite rejections, but I'm not giving up easily. After we have all the questionnaires returned, Tom will do an initial analysis and narrow the search to three. I'll do the same thing, and we'll debate our choices. We might choose the same ones."

Gayle took a deep breath. "I'd like very much to read the

questionnaires and pick three myself. Then I could join the debate."

"Great," Landon said and smiled. "We could use a lawyer's opinion."

"And a proofreader's opinion," Gayle said and patted the envelope. "I'd better get started on these."

"I have a dilemma," Landon said. "I want you to read those, and I want you to stay longer."

"And you can't have both, especially if I'm to have these done by Friday. I'll come another time for a tour of the rest of the house." Gayle walked out into the entry and reached for her coat.

A bundled up Landon and Gayle stepped out into the bitter cold January night.

"How much more of this cold are we going to have? Marta told me you don't have much snow here, yet I heard we might have more tonight." She could see her breath in the light from the street lamp as they walked down the sidewalk to her apartment.

"We usually have two or three snows, one or two inches at a time. A four-inch snow would paralyze this town. But it looks to be an unusual winter. Yes, a very unusual winter," he said looking down at her.

He took Gayle's key and unlocked her door, stepping aside for her to enter. He didn't wait to be invited, but followed her in. Without a word he walked over to the fireplace, opened the door, stirred the coals, and added wood.

"If you'll open the door for me, I'll bring in enough wood to fill your log holder." He strolled briskly out onto the porch.

Gayle watched through the windows of the french doors and gauged the time to open and shut them as Landon quickly carried an arm load to the fireplace. He repeated the procedure four more times, stacking wood on the hearth after the log holder was full.

"That should hold you for awhile. If we do get that snow tonight, you won't be stuck with wet wood." He brushed wood chips off his coat onto the neatly stacked logs.

"Thanks," she said.

"Listen, Gayle, why don't I give you a ride tomorrow? I'll bring you home after your racquetball game with Richard. If the snow comes, no need in both of us sliding around in it."

"No, that's true. I'd appreciate a ride."

"I'll be here at ten till seven so we can have breakfast in the Union," he told her.

seven

Gayle had read four chapters of Landon's galleys when Marta called.

"I have a great favor to ask," Marta started without saying hello.

"Name it," Gayle said.

"Ted is thinking of running for city council. And he'd be great at it. We need responsible people in city government."

"I agree. And he seems like the conscientious type who would do his homework on issues and make sound decisions," Gayle said. "So what's the favor?"

"Would you head up his campaign? Don't say anything yet," Marta hastened on before Gayle could answer. "Think about it. It wouldn't blow your cover. Your background doesn't have to come into it. But you know so much about the process. With you behind him, he'd win for sure."

"Is he paying a filing fee or petitioning for the ballot?" Gayle asked.

"Petitioning. He said if he couldn't get two hundred signatures, he wouldn't have the votes to get elected."

That decision told Gayle that Ted would be a working candidate.

"I'm busy tomorrow after work, but I could meet with

him on Wednesday evening. How does that sound?"

"You mean you'll do it?" Marta asked.

"Of course I'll do it. I miss the excitement of a campaign. This will be fun. I'm unfamiliar with the issues here. Have Ted draw up a list and we'll discuss them and where he stands on each one. That'll dictate what direction we go."

"Oh, Ginny, I mean, Gayle, thank you, thank you. He's so special."

"I know. I think so, too. He'll be a great councilman. Why don't you two come over Wednesday night right after work? We'll order a pizza and pound out the details."

"Great. Wait until I tell Ted!"

"Oh, Marta. What exactly are you going to tell Ted? I mean, will he wonder why you've asked me?"

"I'll just tell him you've worked on a campaign before. I don't want to lie to him."

"I know," Gayle said, thinking of her discussions with Landon. She felt better now that he knew she didn't want to talk about her background. "You can tell him that I'm a lawyer. Landon knows that. But don't tell him why I'm here. Just tell him I needed some time to sort out some things. Fair enough?"

"I can handle that. We'll see you Wednesday. And thank you, thank you."

"No more thank yous. It'll be fun. Bye, Marta."

A campaign to run. She'd never been in charge of one, just in on all the speeches and some of the back room politicking that went on. She'd told Marta the truth. It would be fun. And stimulating. And exciting.

A wave of homesickness washed over Gayle, and she reached for the phone again and punched in her father's private number. He answered on the second ring.

"Hi, Dad."

"Ginny, I've been worried about you. How are things going?"

"Didn't Mom tell you about my job?" Gayle asked. She had called home over the weekend and given her Mom her new address and phone number.

"Yes, she mentioned the university. Are you ready to come home? We miss you."

"I miss you, too. But I'm committed to stay until the end of the semester, the middle of May. Dad, Marta's boyfriend is running for city council and I'm going to run his campaign. Any hints?"

"Can't stay out of politics, Ginny? I know it gets in the blood. City council, heh? That takes me back to my first election. Let me think." He paused a moment and started rattling off procedures Gayle should follow. She reached for a scratch pad and jotted down notes.

"This is just what I needed," she told him. "Thanks."

"Ginny, your mom and I'd like to come visit. Maybe next month. Kentucky plays Arkansas. Can you get us some tickets to the basketball game?"

Gayle sucked in her breath. "Sure, Dad. I'll check on it." She rang off and collapsed in front of the fire.

"Oh, what a tangled web we weave," she said. She hadn't told her dad that she was using her middle name and not trading on the family's position in Kentucky. She had cooked that scheme up on the drive to Arkansas. If he showed up at a ball game, reporters would naturally follow. Not that he was known in Arkansas, but his public relations man would naturally set up some sort of rivalry story and probably get Arkansas's governor up here for the game.

She poked the fire harder than necessary and added another log.

"Dear God, I have so much to sort out. And I have galleys to read," she said out loud. She called Marta back and gave her a list of information they needed for their Wednesday meeting. Then for another hour she sat at the table, blocked out the problems pressing on her, and immersed herself in Landon's words, admiring his turn of phrase, his insights into situations, and his thorough research. Notes at the back of the manuscript documented his sources.

She might have misjudged his earlier works, she thought, and decided to get those books and reread them with an open mind. But for now her eyes were getting heavy.

She stoked the fire before peeking out the window. No snow yet. Maybe the storm would go north of them.

In bed, she held her nightly talk with God, explaining why she had made some recent decisions and asking for guidance in getting out of the hole she was digging deeper and deeper.

When the alarm went off the next morning, Gayle reached a sleepy hand out to silence it. Snuggling back under the blankets felt so warm and comfortable that she wanted to stay longer, but her eyes flew open as she remembered her breakfast date with Landon.

She threw off the covers, jumped out of bed, padded barefoot to the window, and looked out on a carpet of white. She couldn't gauge the depth from the small window, so crossed to the dining area window and looked out at her car. The snow didn't quite reach the hubcap. Not a deep snow, but she was still glad Landon was driving her to school. Although a competent driver, Gayle regarded herself as a menace to the public after a snow. As a teenager, she had slid into a ditch during a snowstorm, and a nagging fear had stayed with her.

Gayle showered and dressed in gray slacks and a burgundy blazer. She stuffed her tote bag with the necessary racquetball equipment, clothes, and some makeup. By a quarter till seven she was watching out the window for Landon's car. When she saw him back out of his drive, she locked her apartment and walked gingerly out to the road so he wouldn't have to turn into her driveway. He pulled up to the curb and reached over and opened the door for her. After kicking her boots against the door frame to shake off the snow, she climbed in beside him and tossed her tote in the back seat.

"Hi," she said.

"Good morning, Gayle." He leaned over and gave her a quick kiss on the lips. It seemed normal for him to greet her like that. "It's a pretty snow."

"It sure is. I'm a good third of the way through the galleys, Landon, and you have a terrific book."

"Thanks. Have you come up with a title yet?" he asked without taking his eyes off the road. He followed the ruts down the middle, probably left by the paper carrier.

"I'm still thinking on that."

It took twice as long as usual to drive to the university and was after seven when he parked the car in the faculty lot. The brisk walk to the Union over freshly shoveled walks reminded Gayle of the day she had interviewed for her job.

"Do you remember the first time we saw each other?" she asked softly.

"Yes. In the parking lot. I wondered what a woman like you was doing here."

"That was a week ago today."

"Impossible," he protested. "Was it really?"

"Seems like we've known each other a lot longer than that," she said.

They had reached the Union, and Landon held the door for Gayle. The heat from the building hit her in the face.

As they walked to the cafeteria, Gayle took off various layers of outerwear: knit cap, scarf, gloves, and heavy coat. Landon laid his coat and scarf in a chair, and Gayle piled hers on top. They moved quickly down the breakfast line, making their selections.

"Can you really eat all that first thing in the morning?" she asked him when they were seated.

"I like a big breakfast, then I taper off on the rest of the meals."

Gayle took a nibble of her cinnamon roll. "Did you play sports in school?"

He acted as if her off-the-wall question was perfectly normal. She was curious about him. He considered that a good sign.

"In high school I played football, basketball, and golf. In college I played basketball, but I wasn't as tall as the other players, so I warmed the bench. These days most of the players approach seven-foot."

"Arkansas has a tall team," she said. "How can I get tickets to a basketball game?"

"I didn't know you were a fan."

"My folks may come for a visit, and my dad would like to see a game. The Kentucky game seems a good choice."

"It'll be a great game. Kentucky made it to the Final Four last year. Good thing we're in the new field house. Barnhill didn't have enough seats for the fans."

Gayle nodded, her mind vaguely registering that the Final Four had something to do with a national tournament.

"So is the ticket office in the new gym?" she asked, still fishing for information.

"Yes, but you can't get tickets until the week of the game. Why don't I pick up four tickets? I'd like to meet your folks."

Gayle took a deep breath and let it out slowly. "Yes, that would be nice," she finally said. By the end of February she'd surely have this mess figured out. Maybe her dad wouldn't mind coming to town incognito. And maybe Arkansas chickens could fly.

She glanced at her watch. "Landon, I've got to run. It'll take me ten minutes to walk to the office."

He looked down at his plate, which still held two pancakes and half an egg. "Could you be late for once?"

"No. Go ahead and finish. I'll see you pretty soon. And

thanks for breakfast." She grabbed her coat and struggled into it as she walked out of the cafeteria. She jammed her cap on, wound her scarf around her neck, and stuck her hands in her pockets.

She arrived at the history office out of breath, but just in time to hear the phone ring as she jammed the key into the lock. She answered on the second ring.

"Good morning, history department," she said into the receiver.

"Gayle, this is Dr. Webber. I'm going to be a little late this morning. The car won't start, so I've got the charger warming the battery. I'm expecting a student at my office right now—Michael Evans. Please tell him I'm delayed and he can either wait a half hour or I'll reschedule our meeting."

"Is your appointment book on your desk and would you like me to reschedule?"

"That would be fine. If he can wait, give him the material in the folder marked 'graduate assistants-library research' that's in your tan filing cabinet."

Gayle assured him that she'd take care of it, replaced the receiver, and walked out into the hall toward Dr. Webber's office. A man who looked to be about her age, dark hair sticking out from under a stocking cap, physique hidden under a down-filled ski jacket, leaned against the wall by the door.

"Hi. Michael Evans?"

"Yes," he said and nodded.

Gayle explained Dr. Webber's message, and together they walked back to the history office. After hanging up her coat, Gayle found the file and gave it to Michael. He was the talkative sort and was soon telling Gayle that he was from Colorado and relating stories of deep snows in the mountains and ski weekends.

Somehow they got on the topic of foreign films, and Michael told her about the weekly movies in the fine arts auditorium.

"Maybe you'd like to go with me sometime?" he asked.

"We'll see," Gayle said. She smiled across the desk at him to soften her gentle refusal and out of the corner her eye caught movement in the doorway.

A scowling Landon stalked into the office, marched over to his mailbox, and took out a memo. "Good morning, Michael," he said brusquely. "May I help you with something?"

"No, Dr. Windsor. I'm waiting for Dr. Webber."

"Dr. Webber phoned to say he was having car trouble and would be in as soon as possible," Gayle explained.

"I see. You left your gloves at breakfast, Gayle." he said, walking over to the coat rack. He removed them from his pocket and slipped them into the pocket of her coat, making it seem like an intimate gesture.

He took off his coat, sat down in the chair beside Michael, and proceeded to discuss a bibliography assignment with the graduate student.

Gayle watched him curiously. What had happened to change his easy attitude from this morning? Landon was back to that aloof professor persona she had noticed the first day she had met him.

Left out of the conversation, she turned her attention to

her projects for the day and started on a test for Dr. Farrell. That woman was thoughtful. The date of the test was February twenty-fourth, and this was the last week in January. She didn't leave anything for a last minute rush.

Fifteen minutes later, Dr. Webber burst into the room. He took Michael to his office, leaving Gayle and Landon alone.

"Does every man you meet ask you out?" he asked.

"No," she answered. What was he driving at?

"When did you meet Michael?"

Gayle glanced at her watch. "Twenty-four minutes ago."

"Fast work, Gayle. When are you going to the foreign film festival?"

"I believe I turned the man down. Landon?" She looked at him curiously. Was he jealous?

Abruptly he turned. "I've got to get to work," he said and left the office.

Landon could have kicked himself all the way down the hall. He'd felt threatened when he'd heard Michael offer to take her to a movie. He had no claim on her. Why should he feel so possessive? And it wasn't just this morning. Why had he made sure that he was included as a spectator in Richard's racquetball game tonight with Gayle?

He unlocked his office and took a seat behind his desk. "Lord," he said. "I don't want to be jealous of her. I want to trust her. But I want to be the only man to kiss her, to hold her."

He didn't distrust her, but he wished he knew more about her past. Something niggled at the back of his memory. He knew something else about her, but he couldn't place it. He mused about it until another professor came in to visit over a cup of coffee.

Gayle worked hard all morning and was ready for a break when Annie came in, full of questions about Dr. Windsor and the office romance.

"We had a nice dinner, and I'm reading his galley proofs," Gayle said.

"And you had breakfast with him in the Union," Annie supplied.

"This is a big university. How do you know so much so fast?"

"My roommate was in the cafeteria," Annie informed her. "And tonight you play racquetball with Dr. Swann. Following your life is better than watching a soap opera."

"Thanks," Gayle said. When she'd been in Kentucky, she'd lived in a fish bowl with her every move scrutinized by the press. Now the student network had taken the place of inquisitive reporters.

"I'll be back," Gayle said. Instead of going to the Union for lunch, she headed for the parking lot and Landon's car. She'd forgotten her tote bag.

"Rats," she muttered when she discovered the car doors were locked and her cold walk had been for nothing. She trekked back to the history building and hoped Landon would be in his office.

His door was open. She stood in the doorway for a moment taking in the scene before her. Landon was sitting at his desk, an attractive blonde woman of around thirty leaning over his shoulder looking at the paper he was reading, her arm lying familiarly on his back.

Landon looked up, his eyebrows raised in question.

"Sorry to bother you, Landon, but could I borrow your car keys? I left my tote bag in the back seat." She took great pleasure as her words wiped the smile off the blonde's face, and the woman leveled a venomous look at Gayle.

"Of course, Gayle." He introduced the two women but didn't offer an explanation as to who Dianne Steele was.

"It's nice to meet you, Dianne," Gayle said automatically and extended her hand.

"Thank you," Dianne replied in a gravelly voice. Although she shook hands, she quickly withdrew her own as if she didn't want to touch Gayle.

Landon dug in his pocket, then handed his keys to Gayle.

"Don't bother returning them. I'll be going to lunch in a moment and I'll stop by your office on my way back into the building. I'm looking forward to this evening. Shall we grab a sandwich after the game?"

"Fine," Gayle said and flashed a smile and a quick wink at Landon. "Nice to have met you, Dianne."

Dianne did not respond with so much as a nod, but turned her attention back to Landon as if they hadn't been interrupted.

Gayle mentally skipped out of the building although she maintained a sedate pace as she again walked to the faculty parking lot. Her analytical mind replayed the scene in Landon's office and the one earlier in her own office. Landon had been jealous that morning. Just as she had been when she had seen him with Dianne.

He had slipped her gloves in her coat as a way of

announcing he was seeing her. She had told Dianne that her tote was in his car for the same reason. And Landon had asked her to dinner right in front of the woman, reassuring Gayle that they were a couple. There was no need for either one of them to feel jealousy. A definite attraction existed between them, and they both knew it. She would relax and enjoy their relationship and let it take what course it would.

Annie was bent over the computer when Gayle popped back into the history office. She stashed her tote bag in the corner and hung up her coat. It was too late to walk over to the Union for lunch.

"Annie," she said, "I'm going to the vending machine for a snack? Care for anything?"

"Sure," Annie said and grabbed her purse. "I'll take a Coke."

"My treat," Gayle called as she started out the door.

In record time she was back, carrying two cans of pop and a package of potato chips.

"Annie," she said, after opening the package and offering some to her assistant. "Who's Dianne Steele?"

"Dr. Steele teaches sociology. She's after Dr. Windsor."

Gayle looked at her thoughtfully. "You don't miss much, do you?"

Annie shrugged. "I saw her come into the building. Her office is in the other wing in social sciences, where Dr. Windsor's should be. Last summer he moved over here so he could have a private office to write in. If you want my opinion, he just wanted to get away from her."

"I see," Gayle said.

Annie grinned. "This really is better than a soap opera."

eight

Richard was waiting at the gym when Gayle arrived after work for their racquetball game. Bundled against the cold, she had not hurried over but had taken her time walking across campus. Large mall areas that had been undisturbed pristine white earlier that morning were now trampled and gray as students had struck across the open areas instead of sticking to the cleared sidewalks.

Man destroys nature's beauty once again, she thought, and her mind turned toward home. Her father had a proposed environmental program in the state legislature. She would ask him about the progress the next time she talked with him.

At the gym, she quickly changed clothes and volleyed with Richard to warm up. His form was not as good as Landon's, she noticed, and his strokes tended to be choppy.

Her gaze traveled of its own accord to the glass partition high on the back wall where spectators could observe the game. The tall blond professor was up there, at the moment talking to a couple of students, but he was there, waiting to see her, to talk to her.

A smile she couldn't control burst across her face like the sun coming up in the morning. Her radiant expression did not escape Richard, who stared at her for a long moment then glanced at the gallery partition.

"You two really have it bad, don't you?"

Gayle looked at him warily, but answered truthfully. "He's a wonderful person, kind, understanding, thoughtful, certainly handsome. . . ."

"All right, I get the picture," Richard interrupted, grinning across at her. "Let's play so you can go out with your knight in shining armor."

Their game went quickly, although some of the opening rallies were long because they were evenly matched. In the end, Gayle's cool head and level strokes gave her the game. Richard lost his concentration when he got behind.

The two opponents shook hands and Gayle looked up at the gallery. Landon gave her the thumbs up sign and she returned it triumphantly.

Gayle quickly showered and dressed, taking time for a light application of makeup, mascara, and lipstick. She sprayed a mist of perfume on her pulse points, packed her tote bag, and headed for the dressing room door.

Her hand was on the handle when she heard through the transom, "Dr. Windsor, you hanging out by the women's locker room these days?" followed by male laughter. The voice probably belonged to one of the students she had seen in the gallery.

"It's as good a place as any for meeting women, wouldn't you say?" Landon replied.

Gayle didn't wait for any further conversation but opened the door to see Landon and a handful of the Razorback basketball team. She hadn't realized there was a crowd or she would have waited for them to move on. As it was, she walked to Landon's side, aware of the six pairs of male eyes watching her.

Landon reached for her tote with one hand and put the other on her shoulder, branding her for the others to see.

"Hey, guys, I'm hanging around here to see what else comes out of there," one of the players announced and squatted down opposite the door to stalk the quarry.

"I've already got the prize," Landon said and guided Gayle to the lobby.

Richard was waiting for them.

"How about a rematch next week?" he asked.

"You'll have to ask my manager," Gayle replied. She didn't want to do anything to spark that jealous feeling in Landon again, now that she had experienced it herself.

"Well?" Richard turned to Landon as the trio walked toward the outside door.

"I believe my client needs a few more lessons from her pro before I'll let her schedule a rematch. She has a busy calendar this month. Matter of fact, she's booked at least until the end of the semester." He was talking to Richard, but Landon's gaze rested on Gayle.

Richard looked from one to the other. "Hey, am I in the way here?"

"Don't be silly, Richard. Landon was just teasing," Gayle was quick to respond.

"I was?" Landon said and held the door for the others.

"Yes, you were."

"What about the faculty dinner Saturday?" Richard asked.

"I haven't had a moment to ask her since I read the memo

this afternoon," Landon said. "Will you go with me, Gayle?"

"I'd love to." She'd read the memo Annie had typed and wondered if Landon would ask her, feeling confident that he would. Since they had had their rounds of jealousy today, their relationship had reached a new level of understanding.

"You two came together?" Richard asked as Landon unlocked the car door for Gayle.

"We're neighbors," Gayle explained. "Landon gave me a ride to school this morning because of the snow."

"Got it bad," Richard said and waved as he continued on to his car.

Landon picked up some hamburgers at the drive-in window at McDonalds and they ate them at Gayle's kitchen table.

"One cup of coffee and you're out of here," she told him as she put on a pot while Landon laid up a fire. "I want to work on those galleys again. Tomorrow night Marta and Ted are coming over, so I won't have time to read then." She explained about Ted running for city council.

"He'll be a good candidate. Could I help? I know quite a bit about campaigns." He lit the gas starter.

"I'm sure you could contribute a lot," Gayle said.

"I have a basketball game at five, but I can be here around six-thirty." Landon stood in front of the fire and stared at the flames licking the wood. "I think I build more fires here than I do at home."

"And you're very good at it," Gayle said and laughed. She carried two cups of coffee to the living room area.

"Why don't I give you a ride again tomorrow morning?" Landon asked.

"Do you need to go in early?"

"Yes. I've got some letters to answer that I'll bring in for you to type, if you have the time. They are for my next book, so aren't strictly university business."

"Dr. Webber told me that getting his professors published is very important, so I'll be glad to help," Gayle said and wondered if the letters regarded the questionnaires he had already received.

They were. She flipped through them the next day at work and found nothing for her father. All the letters were thank yous for responses received in the last two weeks. Gayle had written to Landon shortly before leaving Kentucky. His reply had probably reached the State House after she had resigned her job.

She was tempted to phone Wayne Harvest, her replacement as the governor's aide, and ask if he'd received anything from Dr. Landon J. Windsor, but decided against it. She didn't need to call attention to an already done deal. She had left a clearly marked folder regarding the proposed book by Landon in the filing cabinet. Surely Wayne had asked his secretary to file the follow-up letter and that was the end of it.

Gayle had stayed up late the night before, finishing Landon's galley proofs. She had handed them to him when he had picked her up that morning. Now she was tired from too little sleep, yet keyed up about meeting Marta and Ted that evening and getting back into the political arena.

When Landon dropped her at her house after work and

returned to the campus to play basketball at the church, Gayle changed clothes and headed straight for the grocery store. The main roads were clear, and she had no trouble driving on the side streets that still had patches of ice and snow.

Before her friends arrived around six, Gayle had made a salad and paid the delivery man for two large supreme pizzas, which she popped into a warm oven. She'd made a list of possibilities for political exposure and was setting the table for four when Ted and Marta arrived.

"Ted, I think this is a tremendous decision you've made," Gayle said. "Congratulations."

"I haven't won yet," he said.

"But giving your time and effort to public service is an achievement, whether you win or not. And we're going to make you very visible, which is the key to winning any election."

"Marta said you'd ramrod this thing," Ted said.

"And I'm right," Marta said. "Pizza smells good."

"Landon will be here any minute, and we can eat and talk." Gayle gathered her notes and a pen and placed them beside her place at the table.

But it wasn't until after Landon had arrived and the last slice of pizza had disappeared that they began mapping out the campaign. Gayle cleared the table, but placed a pitcher of iced tea and fresh glasses at each place.

"Looks like a conference," Marta said.

"It is," Gayle said. "We have work to do. First things first. Did you draw up a list of supporters, Ted?"

He handed her a list which had her name at the top.

"Does anyone jump out at you as the one to head your committee as treasurer?"

"Yes. Will you do it?" Ted asked.

"I'd be glad to, but it would be better if you had someone who's influential in the community. Every commercial will end with your committee title and treasurer's name."

Landon looked over the list and made a couple of suggestions. Marta added her two cents worth.

"Okay. If we've decided on Roy Falcon, go ahead and call him, Ted." She motioned toward the phone. "He'll be responsible for handling all the campaign contributions, which we hope will be sizable. However, he won't have to head this committee. So he won't be overworked."

While Ted made the call, Gayle shifted her attention to Marta.

"Did you make a list of the civic clubs and get their presidents' names?"

"Yes, boss." She whipped a list out of the folder she'd brought in with her.

"We need a letter asking if Ted can speak to their membership. Landon will you draft a quick letter? Brief and to the point. Ted would only take ten minutes of their meeting time."

"She is bossy, isn't she?" he asked Marta.

"Yes, but she's good," Marta defended her friend.

Landon turned his attention to the paper in front of him and concentrated on writing a concise letter.

"Marta," Gayle asked, "did you call printers about yard signs?"

"Yes. The figures are in here somewhere." Again she

dug into her file folder. "Here."

Gayle studied the list. "Looks like R and H Printing is low bid. How many did you calculate we'd need?"

"We've got a treasurer!" Ted announced triumphantly as he took his seat again. "He said he'd drop by pretty soon to meet you all."

Landon extracted his checkbook from the inside pocket of his sports coat. "I'll start the campaign off. Then Roy can set up the account." He wrote a check for a hundred dollars and handed it to Ted.

"Landon, I really appreciate this. If you ever need a favor, but not one that deals with the city," he quickly amended, "just ask."

"Corrupt already," Marta said and laughed.

"Unfortunately it begins with something just like that," Gayle said. "I'd watch that phrase, Ted. Some people might misinterpret it." She poured herself a glass of iced tea. "Now. Back to the yard signs, Marta. Did you get the list of registered voters by precinct? Can we gauge how many yard signs from that?"

They agreed on a number and turned their attention to Landon's letter. With a few changes, they agreed it was ready for the computer.

"Feel free to use my study, Gayle. The computer's at your disposal," Landon offered.

"Thanks. That will help. Now, about the slogan. I've only come up with one that might be catchy enough. 'Say Yes to Novak.' We should capitalize on the negative sound of your name before the opposition does. What do you think?"

"It's great," Ted said. "Say Yes to Novak! We'll put it on the yard signs and on business cards. And as the letterhead for our letters. Any other place I've forgotten?"

"Buttons? Some people collect them, so a few wouldn't be out of line. They're not that expensive if we rent a button machine. We could get a few people together and make five hundred of them in an afternoon," Gayle said. "Now, the letterhead. Marta?"

With her artistic flare, Marta took over the meeting, showing logos she'd designed and the different print styles they could use.

"Are we in agreement that this is the best one?" Gayle asked. Everyone nodded. "Ted, this is your campaign. You have to feel comfortable with it. Anytime I'm getting out of line, just tell me."

"Gayle, you're the best thing that's happen to me, politically, that is." He smiled at Marta. "Otherwise I'd have to go with your friend here." He reached over and patted Marta's hand. Marta looked at Ted, and Gayle could see the love in their eyes.

Roy Falcon dropped by, and Gayle and Ted each wrote out a check as a contribution.

"You must keep a total of how much each person has donated for the fair disclosure law on campaign contributions," Gayle told Roy. "It would be best if you'd make a duplicate copy of each deposit slip and give it to Ted or me."

"You really know how to run a campaign," Landon said, a question in his eyes. Her expertise surpassed his expectations by a mile.

"I think I told you that I've always been fascinated by campaigns. I've worked on a few," was all Gayle volunteered.

The meeting went on for another hour with decisions made on information Ted had researched. They discussed the issues and his stand. Gayle and Landon took copious notes which Gayle told him they would combine later and use to come up with some ideas for Ted's speeches and the ads.

"If we put our heads together, we can create some dynamic ads. We won't have the funds to hire an agency. But for a local election, we won't need slick and glitz," Gayle said, falling back into election vernacular.

"This is Wednesday. Let's talk over the weekend, say Saturday afternoon, and see how the petition drive is going. It would be great if you could file on Monday. Meanwhile, Ted, make a file on each issue. Spend time at the library and read back issues of the newspaper. Besides news and features, check letters to the editor. You must know everything there is to know about the issues."

"Didn't I tell you she was good?" Marta said proudly as she carried glasses to the dishwasher.

"Marta, why don't you be the first to sign this petition?" Ted said. "That'll bring me luck."

Marta beamed and scurried to the table to sign her name. She handed the pen to Gayle.

"I can't sign. I'm not a registered voter. I planned on voting absentee at home, but perhaps I can register here if there isn't a long residency requirement. I'll check into it."

"I'll sign," Landon said.

After Marta and Ted left, Landon folded a petition and slipped it into his pocket. "We can get fifteen to twenty names in our building,"

"Good. I forgot to ask. How did the basketball game go?"

"The Hedgehogs won. We're tied for first place with the Eagles."

"Hedgehogs? That's rather unique."

"Somebody's girlfriend thought it was cute. Sort of a play on the Razorback Hogs. Speaking of titles, you didn't name my manuscript. Any ideas?"

"I've given that some thought. What about *Move to the Back of the Bus: The Story of the Civil Rights Movement.* That gives both a catchy phrase and a description of the book and by using the word 'story' it sounds as if it's written in an entertaining style. Which it is. But that may be too long," Gayle added. She didn't want him feeling obligated to suggest it to his editor.

"I like it," Landon said. "I like it a lot."

"My editor likes it," Landon announced to Gayle Friday morning in her office. "She just called and says it's perfect. She presented it to the committee yesterday and it passed. Thanks."

"I'm glad," Gayle said and felt pleased with herself.

"And here's Ted's petition." He presented it with a flourish. "Sixty-four names."

"How did you get that many?" Gayle exclaimed.

"I sat in the Union cafeteria for an hour and asked registered voters to sign. Most of our non-traditional students are local residents."

Gayle immediately called Ted with the news. Although with Landon's petition he had obtained enough signatures to file that afternoon, Gayle advised him to wait until Monday afternoon.

"That way your announcement will coincide with the city council meeting. Your name will be tied with it automatically."

"You're shrewd," Ted said.

"I'd rather think of it as political savvy," Gayle said. "After you file, we'll meet again and go over the issues and finalize committee decisions."

Landon listened to the conversation with interest. Gayle was politically astute. Even knowing there was an advantageous time to file ranked her above an amateur dabbling in politics.

"Gayle?" he started a question, then thought better of it. He'd told her he would wait until she was ready to confide in him. He would keep that promise.

Saturday evening as Landon drove her to Dr. Webber's for the faculty party, Gayle mentioned Ted's campaign.

"He's filing Monday, and we're going to meet again on Tuesday night to finalize some plans. Want to join us?"

"Be glad to. How about some racquetball on Monday? I have a court."

"Pretty confident," Gayle said.

"Yes," he replied as he parked the car on the street. "Looks like we're about the last to arrive. The older faculty members usually arrive a bit early. The youngest, meaning Richard, is always fashionably late."

"And what about you?"

"Punctual," he said and smiled. He climbed out and walked to her door, giving her his hand to help her out and holding it as they walked up the long drive to the Webber's large Tudor home.

Dr. Webber opened the door to their knock and ushered them in, taking their coats. "Introduce Gayle around, Landon. Everyone's here but Richard."

They wandered into the large living room where several groups were assembled. Dr. Farrell introduced her husband to Gayle, and while they exchanged small talk, Landon excused himself to get them each a cup of punch.

"So, you've done the impossible and been out with Landon," Dr. Farrell said with a twinkle in her eye. To her husband she added, "Landon doesn't date anyone from the university. Well, until now."

"I can see why he made an exception with Gayle," Mr. Farrell said.

"Thank you, Mr. Farrell," Gayle replied.

"Oh, please call me John."

"Yes, and call me Sara. I've been meaning to ask you to, but I only see you when there's a crowd in the office." Again she turned to John. "Since Gayle came to work, our male students hang around the bulletin board outside the department office or ask Gayle if they can use her pencil sharpener—all kinds of inventive reasons to talk to her."

Landon was back and handed Gayle a cup. "I've noticed that myself, Sara," he said, having heard her remark as he joined them. "How can we keep those young fellows away from her? I'm sure it cuts down on her productivity."

"I don't think her productivity is what's bothering you,

my friend," Sara teased him.

"You're absolutely right," he said and grinning, put an arm possessively around Gayle's shoulders.

Richard and his date arrived at that moment and joined their group. Sheila Nichols, an attractive brunette in her mid-twenties, knew Landon and the Farrells and greeted them enthusiastically. When she was introduced to Gayle, she shook her hand warmly. Gayle immediately liked her.

"This obviously isn't your first faculty party," Gayle said.

"No, I came to the fall social event, too," Sheila explained. "But you know everyone here, don't you? Rich said you work at school."

"Oh, I know the professors, but not their spouses. It'll be interesting meeting their other halves and seeing if they are anything like I've imagined."

Richard stepped in front of Gayle and blocked her view of the room. With his hands on her shoulders, he turned her to face the wall.

"What are you doing, Richard?" Gayle asked.

"How many couples have you already met?" he asked.

"Just the Farrells," she answered.

"Ladies and gentlemen," he called in a good imitation of a circus ringmaster. "All of you haven't met our new department secretary, Gayle Johnson." Gayle started to turn around, but he kept her staring at the wall. "All the men move over here," he said and motioned to the left side of the room, "and all the women, over here."

"What are you doing, Richard?" Gayle muttered just loud enough for him to hear.

"Just having a little fun. Relax. You can turn around now."

Gayle twirled around and looked at the sea of faces that were staring at her. She glance uneasily at Richard, saw the big grin on his face, and shook her head.

"Hello." She raised her hand in a friendly wave, wishing Richard would get to the point of his little game at her expense. She glanced hopefully at Landon, but he merely shook his head as if he didn't know what was going on, either.

"Gayle just remarked that she was eager to meet the other halves of the professors. Let's see just how well she knows them by seeing if she can match the correct spouses." His suggestion met with loud approval.

"Thanks, Richard," Gayle muttered, but fell in with the game and proceeded by singling out Sara Farrell and matching her with John.

"It's best to start out successfully," she said and smiled at the attentive audience. Since John was the only spouse she'd met, she was stumped for a moment. She had seen several people in groups when they had first entered the room, but that didn't necessarily mean they were married. Still she went on the assumption that husbands and wives would stick pretty close together at the beginning of an evening. She picked out Dr. Strausman and successfully matched him with his wife, a big woman who almost matched him in size. She pulled Dr. Anderson out to the center of the floor and then picked a slim redhead as his wife. From the laughter she could tell it was wrong and asked the woman if she was having a good time. The woman answered in the biggest southern drawl, "A wonderful time, sugar."

A light bulb went on above Gayle's head and she pointed to Dr. Talbott. That left her with Dr. Anderson still in the middle of the floor. She walked over to the group of women, said "hello," and listened to them respond. She picked out a petite brunette, knowing that woman's voice had asked to speak to Dr. Anderson on the phone.

She had a good memory for voices and correctly matched the next few couples by asking the women to repeat phrases for her. She was down to the last two men and discovered that Landon had strolled over to join the men's group. She called him to the middle of the floor and tapped her index finger against her chin, as if pondering which of the remaining two women belonged with him.

"Hey, I'm with you, remember?" Landon said and playfully put his arm around her and gave her a helping hand matching the last two couples.

"Well done, Gayle," Dr. Webber said, then announced that the buffet dinner was ready.

The buzz of conversation and laughter filled the room as the group filed into the dining room.

"I've never seen the group mix so well," Landon told Gayle, although Richard took credit for the ice breaking game.

After filling their plates, the youngest foursome found a secluded corner in the den to have their feast. Gayle discovered that Sheila was a nurse at Washington General Hospital.

"Right now I'm working in pediatrics. I like working

with the little ones, but it can be heart-breaking at times."
Sheila warmed to her subject of the children's ward, but
stuck to the amusing incidents instead of the depressing
illnesses.

While they visited, Gayle noticed that Richard was very
possessive toward Sheila, keeping a hand touching her
shoulder or arm. She was going to comment on it to
Landon, when she noticed her hand resting on his forearm
and wondered when she had put it there. She withdrew it
slowly, but Landon reached for it and put it right back
where it had been.

nine

During the next week, Gayle and Landon spent every evening together. They played racquetball twice, worked on Ted's campaign, and worshiped together. Gayle even watched the Hedgehogs defend their number one status against the Eagles. On Saturday night they attended a play at the university and made plans to go to the campus church together the next day.

"I'll provide dinner this time," Gayle told Landon when he took her home that night.

The next morning she was up early and threw on jeans. She straightened her apartment, made a grocery list, and headed for the store. When she came back, still working in fast forward mode, she made lasagna, cleaned vegetables for a salad, and took a shower. After dressing in her favorite red dress with white piping on the sleeves and down the front, she sat down on the couch with a sigh of relief and a cup of coffee, mentally going over the steps she'd take to finish dinner when she and Landon returned from church.

"The bread," she exclaimed. How had she forgotten french bread? She glanced at her watch, calculating the time she'd need to get to the store and back.

In less than twelve minutes, she had driven to the store, bought the bread, and returned.

"Done," she said and brushed her hands together with a sense of accomplishment. She watched out the window for Landon, but he didn't come. The kitchen clock said he was two minutes late, which was nothing, even though he prided himself on his promptness. After five minutes, Gayle's gaze alternated between the window and the clock. Ten minutes later, she set out the short distance to Landon's house.

She walked quickly past the Connor home. By the time she passed the Phillips house, she was jogging in her high heels. She ran up the steps to Landon's front porch. She poked the doorbell and waited a moment. He didn't answer. She poked it again. After another long moment without any sound of movement inside, she tried the doorknob. It turned.

"Landon?" she called, sticking her head inside the door.

She thought she heard a sound upstairs, so closed the door and walked to the foot of the stairs.

"Landon?" she called up the stairwell.

She heard him answer but couldn't make out what he said, so she climbed the stairs with a sudden urgency born of the conviction that something was very wrong.

Gayle found a pale Landon in bed, his eyes half closed. He reached his hand out slowly to draw her to him.

"I called come in, but I guess you couldn't hear me," he said in a weak voice so unlike his usual deep masculine tone.

"Landon, what is it? Are you hurt?" Gayle asked.

"No. I've just picked up a bug somewhere. I started feeling bad this morning and tried a bit of toast and tea, but it didn't stay down. I've vomited a couple more times since then and feel wretched. I tried to call you, but you didn't answer." He looked as if the effort to talk exhausted him.

Gayle placed her palm on his forehead. "Landon, you're burning up with fever. I'll bathe your face."

"No, Gayle. I don't want you to stay. I may be contagious." His voice sounded stronger as he ordered her out.

"I'm not going anywhere, Landon," she called over her shoulder as she dumped her coat in a chair and went into the bathroom. She returned with a damp wash cloth and towel and with soothing motions began bathing his face, his arms, and his hands.

"Where's your thermometer?"

"Bathroom medicine cabinet," he muttered.

She quickly found it and slipped it under his tongue. "Keep it there while I run downstairs a moment." She zipped down the stairs and banged kitchen cabinets in her search for saltine crackers. She found some and took them and a Coke back to the bedroom.

"I want you to try these," she said and took the thermometer. "Landon, your temp is a hundred three and four tenths. We need to get you to a doctor."

"It's Sunday. Where would we go?"

"The hospital."

"No. If I'm not better by morning, I'll go to my doctor. Don't look so worried, I've been sick before."

"I'm sure you have," she said lightly, trying to ease the fear she was feeling. "Try these crackers."

He nibbled on the cracker and swallowed a couple of sips of Coke. "That's all Gayle. It won't stay down. I can already feel the pain in my stomach."

He was right. Within two minutes he was in the bathroom, heaving.

Gayle helped him back to bed and leaned over to tuck the covers around him. She accidently touched his right side, and an involuntary moan escaped him.

Instantly, Gayle was alert. "Landon, does it hurt when I touch here?" She touched the left side of his lower abdomen.

"Yes, I'm sore all over."

"What about this?" She gently pushed on his right side, hoping she was wrong in her diagnosis.

He moaned. "Don't do that," he said. She could see the pain in his eyes.

"Tell me when the pain lessens." She explored the region with her fingers. "Landon," she said when she had completed her examination, "there's a possibility that you have appendicitis. Have you ever had it before?"

"No, Gayle. I have a bug. I'll be better in the morning."

"Yes, you will. We're going to make sure of it. Where's your phone book?"

"In the drawer," he said.

Gayle found the number for Washington General and dialed it.

"Get dressed," she said after she had talked to a nurse. "There's a clinic at the hospital, and the nurse will give you a blood test. Don't start," she said when she saw his reaction to her order. "My mom had an appendicitis attack that we mistook for the flu. She almost died because her appendix burst as they were taking it out and some poison went into her system. If I'm wrong, and I hope I am, then we'll get something to help with your nausea. What can I get you to wear?"

"I can get dressed," he said.

"Fine. I'll be right outside this door if you need me," she said.

Gayle took the crackers and Coke down to the kitchen, then climbed back upstairs and leaned against the wall outside Landon's bedroom.

"How are you doing?" she called.

"Come on in," Landon said.

He was sitting on the bed wearing tan slacks with no belt and a plaid shirt. "Okay, so I'm weak," he conceded. "Could you help me with my shoes? I don't like bending over."

Gayle put on his socks and shoes and held his arm as they went down the stairs.

"Sit here," she directed. "I'll go get my car."

Landon handed her his keys. "Drive mine. Let's just get this over with and get back home."

Within minutes they arrived at the hospital clinic, but it took a full half hour before the forms were filled out and Landon's name was called. Finally he was taken back to the lab. Gayle sat in the waiting room, flipped through an outdated magazine without reading a single word, and walked down the hall and back several times.

God, she prayed silently, *please let him be all right.*

Landon returned and again they sat in the waiting room. He had gotten sick in the lab and looked worse than when they had come in. Another half hour passed while they sat quietly.

"I'd hate to be here with a real emergency," Landon said, looking at the hands on the big wall clock.

"They must be waiting for the lab report," Gayle said. She felt responsible for his irritation since she'd insisted he see the doctor.

At that moment a huge nurse in regimental white called Landon's name and led him through swinging doors and out of Gayle's view.

Again Gayle paced the hall. The unpleasant antiseptic smell of the hospital assailed her nostrils. It was already past noon, and she thought of her lasagna waiting to be stuck in the oven. She bought a can of pop from the vending machine in the waiting room and had just popped the top when the nurse pushed open the swinging doors and called her name. Gayle followed her back to the area where Landon, looking more pale than before, lay on a high examining table.

"Well, Gayle, you were right. The blood test shows it's my appendix, and the doctor's decided it has to come out now. They'll operate in about an hour."

"Mr. Windsor, you'll be in room one forty-three," the rotund nurse said as she was joined by a thinner woman. "Dorothy, take him to his room, but swing by admitting first and get him a bracelet. Tell them the other information is already in the computer. Don't eat or drink anything, Mr. Windsor," she said, glancing at the Coke Gayle was holding.

Gayle followed the thin nurse as she pushed Landon's wheelchair down the hall into the interior of the hospital.

After a quick stop by admitting, they arrived at room one forty-three.

"Mr. Windsor, put this gown on, please. A nurse will be in to shave your stomach in a few minutes. Lab will be up to get some more blood, too." She laid a gown on the single bed and left them.

"Landon, is there someone we should call? Your folks?" Gayle suggested. "I'm sure they'd appreciate knowing."

"All right. Would you phone them?" He told her the number and went into the rest room to put on the gown.

Gayle used the hospital operator to place the call to Seattle and got Landon's mother on the line while he was still in the bathroom.

"Mrs. Windsor, this is Gayle Johnson, a friend of Landon's. . . . Oh, he's fine." She had thought Landon would be out of the bathroom and able to tell his mother about the impending operation, but faced with her concern, she decided to tell Mrs. Windsor herself.

"Actually, Landon's appendix is acting up, and the doctor has decided to take it out this afternoon. . . . Yes, you could call it an emergency operation. He started feeling bad this morning but thought he had a touch of the flu."

She looked up to see Landon come out of the bathroom and lie down on the bed, waiting for the phone.

"I forced him to come," she said into the receiver. "And you're right, Mrs. Windsor. He does like his own way." She laughed and handed Landon the receiver.

"Mother, please don't tell Gayle all my faults, she already knows enough of them. . . . Yes, she's the one

. . . . I have no idea. . . . Washington General. . . ."

Gayle thought he might want a private word with his mother and started to leave, but Landon motioned her back to his side. She helped him up as another wave of nausea hit him and took the phone as he headed for the bathroom.

"Hello, this is Gayle again. Landon is sick in the bathroom. Oh, Mr. Windsor. . . . Yes, very competent. . . . Don't worry. I'll stay with him and call you as soon as it's over . . . . Yes. . . . Good-bye."

Landon teetered out of the bathroom, and Gayle ran to assist him into bed. A nurse came in followed by a lab technician, so Gayle stepped out into the hall to wait. A big man, around fifty, with a balding head and round face, entered the room, stayed a few minutes, then came out and had a word with her.

"I'm Dr. Kellough. The OR is being set up now, so we should be in there within twenty minutes," he said, glancing at his watch. "He should be in recovery an hour after we begin. I'll come to the surgery waiting room as soon as we finish. He's in good physical condition and I foresee no complications, but that appendix must come out. Any questions?"

Gayle smiled at the doctor who exuded confidence. His demeanor told her that this was a routine operation he had performed hundreds of times and that he wanted her to trust him.

"You've answered all my questions," she said. "I'll be waiting to speak with you."

He patted her on the arm. "It'll be over in no time, you'll see," he reassured her, then left her alone in the hall.

Minutes later the nurse and the lab technician came out, and Gayle went back into the room.

"How are you feeling?" she asked anxiously.

"It only hurts when I laugh," he said.

"Oh, Landon. You're going to be just fine. What can I do for you while you're being de-appendicized?"

"Is that a word?"

"It is now. So, what can I bring you? Magazines? Pajamas?" She dug paper and pen from her purse and sat down on the edge of his bed making the list.

"What about school? Shall I call Dr. Webber?"

"I'd forgotten about school. How long do you think I'll be out?"

"I'd guess three or four days in the hospital and at least another week of recovery at home." Gayle watched his brows come together as he considered her words.

"I'll have to get someone to deliver my lectures."

"Where are your notes? Could I do it?" she offered. She'd do anything to ease his mind before he went into surgery.

"Sure you could. I've had lawyers as guest speakers before. My notes are at home in my study, the left hand filing drawer of my desk. I'm teaching four classes this—" He didn't complete his sentence as his teeth clenched together in pain. Gayle reached for his hand, and he squeezed hard.

A moment later the pain subsided. "Are you timing these contractions? I must be in labor," he joked, but Gayle could see the pain still in his eyes.

"You'll make medical history." She was holding his

hand as she leaned over and kissed his brow. Her lips tasted the salt from the sheen of sweat on his skin.

"This thing sure progressed fast since we came to the hospital. Maybe we'd better go back home and I'll feel better," he suggested.

"Not a chance, mister," she said. "Landon, I don't know the chair of the social science department. Will he accept me lecturing for you?"

"Dr. Raymond Bergen. It'll be fine. We don't have to clear our guest speakers with him. Since you'll be lecturing several days, you might introduce yourself to him as a professional courtesy. And you'll have to ask Dr. Webber for time out of the office. You may have to tell him you're a lawyer. How do you feel about that?"

"I don't mind." Gayle had come to the conclusion that she had earned her law degree without the help of her father. It was something she could claim for herself without using the family name.

Gayle leaned down and hugged Landon. "I'm so scared," she confided and immediately regretted admitting her fear for him.

"Hey, I'm the one going under the knife," he said, but held her tightly against his chest.

"I know. I'm sorry I said that."

"I'm not. I'm glad you're scared for me. It means you care."

"You know I do." She nestled closer to him. "But I know God will take care of you."

"Time to go, Mr. Windsor," a nurse called brightly as she and two other nurses brought in a stretcher.

Gayle kissed Landon on the cheek and watched the nurses expertly transfer him from his bed to the gurney.

"Take it easy," she said as she grabbed his hand for one last touch before he was wheeled off. "God be with you."

He nodded briefly and was gone.

Gayle sat down on the empty bed and clasped her hands together. "Dear God," she prayed. "Please be with Landon during this operation. Make him be all right. And help the next hour go quickly."

Gayle swallowed hard to gain control over her taut emotions. She glanced at her watch. One hour, the doctor had said. She decided to explore the hospital, knowing she couldn't sit still that long.

She found the cafeteria but couldn't face the thought of food. She saw the babies in the obstetrics wing, then took the stairs to the next floor.

Drawings of giraffes, elephants, and monkeys lined the walls between room doors. At the nurses' station she saw Sheila, clipboard in her hand, a welcoming smile on her lips.

"What brings you here, Gayle?" she asked.

Gayle explained about Landon.

"Dr. Kellough is one of the finest surgeons on staff. I'm sure Landon's in good hands," she assured Gayle.

"I'm sure he is," Gayle agreed.

"But you're still scared silly."

"Petrified. Does it show?"

"When you love someone, even the simplest operation makes you realize you could lose him. And that's scary."

Gayle didn't deny her love for Landon, but nodded.

Sheila's sympathy had caused the tears Gayle had buried to come very close to the surface.

"I'd better get to the waiting room," she choked out and turned away.

She found the deserted surgery waiting room, sat down by a window, and stared sightlessly at the winter scene beyond. Unconsciously she clasped her hands together and talked again to God, confiding her fears for Landon. She sat with her head bowed, unaware of the minutes ticking by.

"Gayle," a masculine voice said softly as a hand touched her shoulder. She turned to find Richard standing beside her.

"Richard?" Her voice asked the question.

"Sheila called me. He's still in surgery?"

"Yes." She glanced at her watch and was surprised to see the time. "It's been fifty minutes. The doctor said an hour."

She had barely completed the sentence when Dr. Kellough came through the door in his surgical greens. His smile told her all was well before he said the actual words and went on to explain that Landon was in recovery and would be there for a couple hours.

"Thank God," Gayle said.

"Well, that's good news," Richard said after the doctor had left. At his words Gayle's pent up tears were unleashed in a torrent of sobs. Richard hugged her as she cried on his shoulder.

"You must have misunderstood, Gayle. He said Landon was all right." He laughed and Gayle laughed with him, but the tears didn't stop for some time. She had been on such an emotional tightrope, she needed the release to bring her down to reality again.

When she was finally back in control, Richard drove them to Landon's house to pack a suitcase. Gayle called the Windsors, assuring them that their son was fine, and found Landon's lecture notes. She stuck them in the suitcase, too.

On the way back to the hospital, Gayle asked Richard to stop at a fast food Mexican place. All of a sudden she was ravenous, and she ordered three tacos. They sat at a booth while she ate, Richard keeping a running conversation. Gayle was about to broach the subject of calling Dr. Webber when Richard brought it up.

"We need to call Dr. Bergen. He'll have to get a sub for Landon. I could probably give his history lectures, but we need someone for poly sci."

"I told Landon I'd lecture for him. I brought his notes to study this evening."

"Uh, Gayle. . .," Richard started.

"I haven't been completely open about my past," Gayle hastened on before he could question her qualifications to lecture. "I have a law degree and am a licensed attorney in Kentucky."

Her announcement was followed by silence as Richard studied her.

"Where did you go to school?" he finally asked.

"Harvard."

"Wow, you're full of surprises. Does Landon know? But then he'd have to or he wouldn't have agreed to let you teach," he answered his own question.

"Yes, he's known for a while. I took this job for one semester, then I'm going to practice law somewhere." At one time she would have said Kentucky, but now she wasn't so sure she'd return to her home state.

"Does Dr. Webber know?" Richard asked.

"No. I didn't think I'd get the job if I listed all my education. How do you think he'll take it?"

"You've done your job well, so I shouldn't think he'd mind. You may be inundated with questions about the law as soon as everyone knows. Are you ready to go?"

Gayle nodded, stuffed her trash in a container, and took her paper cup with her. When they arrived at the hospital, they walked briskly to Landon's room and found it empty.

"I guess we're a little early," Gayle said and glanced at her watch. She unpacked Landon's bag and stacked the files of notes on the side table. "I'll call Dr. Webber before Landon is brought back."

"I'll go see Sheila. Be back in a few minutes. Good luck," Richard added before strolling out.

Dr. Webber was concerned about Landon and not surprised by Gayle's confession about her education. "I didn't know what you were hiding," he told her, "but I knew you'd had some formal education. It sticks out all over you." He agreed with her suggestion that she lecture for Landon, and Gayle assured him that she would stay after hours if necessary to complete any work the professors had for her, so she wouldn't fall behind in her job.

Next Gayle called Marta, who chastised her for not calling earlier. "I would have come sit with you while you waited for news," her friend said.

"I appreciate that," Gayle said. "I wasn't thinking straight or I would have called. He should be brought back to his room any time. I'll keep you posted."

She looked up Clark Rossiter's number in the phone book and dialed him.

"What's wrong with Landon?" he asked as soon as Gayle identified herself.

"He's fine now," she assured him, "but he's missing his appendix. How did you know something was wrong?"

"He doesn't miss a Sunday unless he's out of town. And he would have told me if he was going somewhere. I've been calling his house and have called your house, too. Is he all right now? Can I see him?"

Gayle explained what she knew and promised to let him know any new developments.

A few minutes later Landon was brought into the room. The nurses transferred him from the gurney to his bed and left instructions for Gayle to call them if he began vomiting.

Landon's skin was gray. It scared Gayle. She sat by the side of the bed holding his hand, glad to feel the warmth of it in her own.

"Thank you, God," she murmured for at least the twentieth time since Landon had been brought back into the room. He was sleeping. She leaned over and kissed him lightly on the cheek.

"A touching scene," Richard drawled from the doorway.

"Don't mind him," Sheila countered as she walked in ahead of him. "I'm on break and thought I'd check our new patient. When did they bring him back?"

Gayle answered their questions and continued to hold Landon's hand tightly in hers. Their voices must have disturbed him, for his eyes blinked several times and stayed open for a moment.

"Gayle." His voice was thick, and he drew out her name.

"I'm right here, Landon. You're doing fine, and I'm right here," she said in a soothing voice.

The corners of his mouth lifted just a little before his eyes rolled back into his head. He was asleep again.

"He'll be like that for a couple more hours until he drops into a normal sleep," Sheila told her.

"What did Dr. Webber say?" Richard asked.

"He approves." She picked up the files of notes. "Landon's extremely organized, so it shouldn't be difficult."

"We'll leave you to it," Richard said. "Unless there's something else we can do to help?"

"No, but I do appreciate your being here. I'll see you tomorrow."

Left alone, Gayle began to sort through the notes. She had only read through Monday's notes for one class when Clark Rossiter walked in.

"I had to see for myself that he was all right," Clark said. "Not that I doubted you," he quickly assured Gayle.

"I understand completely," Gayle said. "He's been in and out of consciousness, but he's breathing more naturally now."

As if on cue, Landon opened his eyes. "Gayle?"

"I'm right here. You have a visitor." She stood up and motioned for Clark to take her place next to the bed.

"Hi, old buddy. What happened to you? One minute you're fine and the next you've checked into this deluxe hotel for some rest."

Landon smiled. "No rest," he said. "Water?"

"I'll check," Gayle said. "Be right back."

When she returned from the nurses' station with a cup of ice chips, Landon was asleep and Clark Rossiter had his head bowed in prayer.

After a moment he raised his head.

"Thanking the Lord that my friend is okay."

"The Lord's had a busy prayer line today as far as Landon's concerned," Gayle said. "And He answered yes to all of mine."

ten

After Clark left, Marta and Ted tiptoed in.

"How's he doing?" Marta asked.

"He's sleeping fine now," Gayle said. She stepped out into the hall to visit with them so they wouldn't disturb Landon.

"Have you eaten supper?" Marta asked. "Could we get you something or go to the cafeteria?"

"I ate a late lunch. Would you stay with him while I get a drink from the vending machine? I don't think he'll need anything, but he can have ice chips if he wants."

Ted stayed with Landon while Marta and Gayle walked to the basement vending area.

"How are you doing?" Marta asked.

"I'm fine now. But when you come close to losing someone, you realize his worth to you." She echoed what Sheila had said earlier.

"Why, Ginny Gayle Johnson. What are you telling me? That you're in love with Landon?"

Gayle dropped two quarters in the pop machine and pushed the button before answering. "I guess that's what I'm saying. I need to think about this. Seems impossible, doesn't it? I've known him less than a month. I don't even know that much about him, just that he's a fine, upstanding

Christian man. He would never use me like Frank did."

"So are you going to tell him who you are?"

"Yes, I'll tell him soon. When he's well again and can take the shock," she said and laughed. "I'd hate to cause him a setback."

After Marta and Ted left, Gayle studied Landon's class notes. Local Government would be easy. She could handle American Presidency, too. Political Philosophy would be somewhat more difficult, but she could handle it. She would strive not to instill her own opinions in her lectures, but concentrate on historical precedents.

Landon's parents called his room, but the phone didn't rouse Landon since Gayle grabbed it on the first ring. Around ten o'clock, a nurse urged Gayle to go home and get some rest, but she was too keyed up to sleep and knew she'd rather be with Landon than at home thinking about him.

But think about him she did. If it were possible to be in love with a man after knowing him such a short time, then she was in love with Landon. The exhilarating feeling she experienced when she was in his arms and the easy, comfortable feeling she had when talking to him added up, in her analytical mind, to love.

She had moved to Arkansas to come to grips with her own self-worth, and she had come a long way. In a few weeks' time, she had established herself very well—she could support herself and had made friends without using family connections. Finding someone to love and who loved her was an added bonus.

But does he love me? she wondered. "Please God, help me find out," she prayed.

Around midnight a nurse came in with a pain killing shot that would put Landon to sleep for several hours. After making sure that he was sleeping soundly, Gayle gathered the class notes and tiptoed out of the room, vowing to return within a few hours.

By six-thirty the next morning, Gayle was back in Landon's room. She watched him sleep fitfully, moving and moaning softly as the movement hurt his incision.

Gayle bent down and kissed him lightly. He stirred, but didn't wake. She sat down and reviewed the lecture notes one more time. If Landon didn't wake soon, she would go to work without talking to him. She shouldn't have worried about that, for a nurse waltzed in and woke Landon so she could take his vital signs.

"Hi," Gayle said to him. "How're you feeling?" She stood up and took his hand in hers.

"I didn't even see the truck that hit me," he mumbled and smiled feebly. He didn't seem surprised to see her.

Gayle laughed. "Are you in much pain?"

"Only when I laugh."

"Then I won't tell you any jokes."

"Could I have a drink?"

Gayle turned to the nurse. "I'll check his chart," she said and left after taking his blood pressure. She returned shortly with a glass and a water pitcher. "Just what the doctor ordered, Mr. Windsor. You'll get some Jello and broth for breakfast. You can pretend you're getting bacon and eggs through that IV tube."

"That'll take a lot of imagination," Landon said and greedily drank from the glass Gayle held for him. She adjusted his bed so he could reach the bed table and told him of yesterday's events.

"Clark was here? And Richard? I don't remember them."

"Do you remember much?"

He grinned sheepishly. "Just you."

"I'm glad you remember me. I'll come by after work. Right now I'd better get going. Rest up today—catch up on daytime television," she teased.

"Right. See you tonight, honey."

He was still a bit groggy, maybe that's why he had called her honey, she told herself on the way to the office. But another voice inside her argued that he meant to call her honey and that it wasn't just another pat phrase used by a carefree bachelor. It was an endearing phrase meant especially for her.

"God, I'm always asking you for favors. But, please make it so."

The day flew by. Gayle scurried from the office to the classroom and back, she told Landon later that evening.

"Dr. Bergen was concerned about you. He was a bit reserved at first, but I soon had him eating out of my hand. He's just a big teddy bear."

"I wouldn't let him hear you say that."

Gayle laughed. "He agreed that I could lecture for you until you're back. Any tips for tomorrow's classes? Political Philosophy looks formidable."

"That's a graduate class, and we have some great discussions. Let Randy Pressman make a statement and then the class will argue the entire period. Just make sure you have control. Be best if you could skim Binford's text before class time. It's in my study on the shelf behind my chair."

"I'll get it when I go home. Any idea when you'll get out of here?"

"None. Too early to tell, the doctor said. But I'm getting stronger fast. Let's walk down the hall. The more I move, the faster I'll go home."

Gayle helped Landon out of bed and into his robe, draping one side over his shoulder because of the IV tube still in his arm.

"I get rid of this tomorrow." He nodded at the intravenous pole he used as a walking stick as they made their way slowly down the hall.

Before they returned to the room, Clark Rossiter joined their parade, and a few minutes later Dr. Webber walked into the room.

Gayle slipped out to speak with the nurse.

"He's been in quite a bit of pain today, but after one pain shot he refused any more. Said it muddled his mind. We're giving him pain pills now, but they are much milder. He's a tough man. And a stubborn one," she said and laughed good-naturedly.

Gayle agreed and returned to Landon's room to find Richard had arrived. When visiting hours were over,

Gayle kissed Landon good-bye and walked out to the parking lot with Richard and Clark.

"How're things going?" Clark asked.

"Hectic. I lectured three classes today besides running the office. I have one test to type tonight. I'm going to use Landon's computer. And he says I should skim a textbook for tomorrow's class." She unlocked her car. "But the pace won't be for long. I'll manage."

On reflection, Gayle didn't know quite how she would manage. She sat in Landon's chair in his study, sipping coffee and skimming Binford's lengthy text. Hours later she glanced at her watch. After midnight. She'd already completed the test, but she was through only a fraction of the textbook.

She reached for the lecture notes and reviewed the limited subject matter. Landon's mind must have been muddled from pain medicine if he thought she could comprehend this text in one night. She would stick to the one topic and read the parts in the book that pertained to it. If Randy Pressman led the class in another direction, she'd channel it back to the topic and tell him to keep that thought for when Dr. Windsor returned.

She told Landon her plan when she saw him at breakfast Tuesday and reported that the class had gone well when she visited the hospital after work. She laughingly mentioned that his star pupil, Randy Pressman, had been absent and that she'd been relieved to see the empty chair.

Clark arrived and they talked while Gayle sat beside Landon, holding his hand. Landon clutched her hand tightly. His head hurt, and he was tired of lying in a hospital bed.

"How about a cup of coffee?" he heard Clark ask Gayle when the chimes announced visiting hours were over.

"Sounds good," Gayle answered. She kissed Landon good-bye, promised to see him the next morning, and walked out of the room with one of his best friends.

Landon pounded on the bed with his fist, which jarred him and made his head feel worse. He needed out of the hospital.

"His IV is out and he's eating regular food," Gayle told Sara Farrell Wednesday morning. "It was nice of you to send him flowers. They cheer up the place." Actually his room looked like a floral shop. Several bouquets and potted plants had arrived the day before.

Gayle had finished Landon's second class and had just collapsed in her office chair when the phone rang.

"Got any plans for lunch?" Landon asked nonchalantly.

"What's up?"

"If you could take a long lunch hour, you could spring me from this place."

"You're being dismissed? Wonderful! I'll talk to Dr. Webber and be right there. Wait, when should I be there?" Her words tumbled over each other.

"The doctor's already signed the release papers, and the business office is getting all the red tape together. By the time you get here, I should be packed and ready."

"Okay. I'll see you soon." She rang off, checked with Dr. Webber, and called and asked Clark if he would go with her. She fairly skipped out to her car where she met Clark.

Landon was coming home. No more trips to the hospital. Just down the block and she could see him. *Thank You, God,* her heart sang as she maneuvered the car into the hospital loading zone.

Gayle was stunned when she saw Landon. He was fully dressed, standing by the window, and she watched him sink wearily into a chair. His face was ashen. Obviously getting dressed and walking around his room unassisted had exhausted him.

"You don't look well enough to leave," she told him.

"I'll be fine. Hello, Clark. Thanks for coming."

"Did the doctor really dismiss you?" Gayle wasn't convinced he should be leaving.

"Yes. He said if I had someone to take care of me, I'd be better off at home. And I agree."

"But you have no one."

"I'll be fine," he said.

"We can set up a baby-sitting schedule," Clark said. Landon glanced at him with disgust. "Members of the church basketball team can rotate in and out. I'll spend the night."

"Okay," Landon growled.

Clark loaded plants on a cart and pushed it ahead of him while Gayle carried Landon's bag. Landon protested that he didn't need a wheelchair, but the nurse insisted he be wheeled out.

"I'm not an invalid," Landon complained.

"I can tell you're going to be a barrel of laughs," Clark said. "How long is this convalescence?" he asked Gayle.

"If he behaves and gets rest, he'll be okay in a week. If he tries too much too early, could be two," she said as she drove them to Landon's house.

Once there, she unlocked the front door and helped Landon inside while Clark began the unloading process.

"Welcome home," she said and felt it was their home she was bringing him into. She had spent the last few nights in his study either at the computer or reviewing his notes.

Landon looked around as if he hadn't seen the house in months, wandering from room to room until Gayle insisted he go to his bedroom.

"Have you found someone to stay?" Gayle asked Clark as she fixed a pitcher of ice water for Landon's bedside table.

"Benny should be here anytime."

"I'll call Mrs. Connor and ask if she can stay a few minutes since we need to get back to work."

"Everything's arranged," Clark told Landon.

"I'll bring dinner over tonight," Gayle told Landon and kissed him before they left.

Landon glanced around his own bedroom and heaved a sigh of relief and exhaustion. Home at last. His eyes closed of their own accord. He opened them a few minutes later and found Mrs. Connor and Benny Bruffet staring at him.

"You okay, Dr. Windsor?" Benny asked. "You need anything?"

"I'm fine, thanks."

"Okay, Dr. Windsor. If you need anything. . . ."

"I'll call," Landon said and squirmed around, trying to find a comfortable position.

He woke up to voices in the hall but kept his eyes closed and listened. The changing of the guard. Unless he missed his guess, Jason Lauderback was replacing Benny.

"Look in on him every fifteen minutes or so and make sure he's breathing," he heard Benny say.

Landon smiled at that. He didn't feel close to death, just close to boredom, and that was not a state he enjoyed. On many occasions he had told his nieces and nephews that if they were bored it was because they weren't thinking. But his mind wouldn't concentrate on much. He'd tried reading in the hospital and couldn't remember what he'd read moments after reading it.

No more pain pills. They were doing this to him. And he wanted a clear mind. While he didn't need to prepare for classes, he'd designate this week off as time for research for his next book.

With that thought in mind, Landon reached for the bedside phone and called his graduate assistant.

"Tom, I'm glad I caught you. Do you have any time tomorrow to come over to my home and review everything we have on the Senate races?" He would give himself the day off to get used to being home again. And time for his mind to clear.

"I'm doing fine. One o'clock is good. I'm not going anywhere. Bring everything you've got and stop by my office and get everything filed under Senate in the second drawer of the filing cabinet. Got that? Gayle in the history office will have the key to my office." He'd have to remember to give it to her.

He felt better after talking to Tom. Now he just needed to get stronger. He pushed himself into an upright position on the side of the bed, rested a moment, then stood up. He wasn't too bad once he got on his feet; it was trying to get upright without putting pressure on his incision that caused him pain.

He tied on his robe and padded barefoot down the stairs, holding onto the bannister for support.

"Hey, Dr. Windsor, you can't come down here," Jason Lauderback greeted him at the foot of the stairs. "You're supposed to call me if you want something."

"I could use a cold drink, but I'll get it. I need to walk."

Landon sat downstairs in the living room for a few minutes, then returned to bed. By the time Gayle arrived, he was ready to sit in the kitchen while she set out a full meal from the Colonel.

"Fried chicken," she announced. "Different from the AQ House, but tasty." She pulled cardboard bowls from a sack. "Potatoes and gravy, slaw, and a biscuit. What would you like to drink?"

"Water is fine." He didn't want to eat or drink. What he really wanted to do was hold Gayle. Or be held by Gayle. He wanted to touch her, to smell the fragrance of her hair.

"You have to eat to get stronger," she said, as if reading his mind. He knew she was right and forced down two pieces of chicken.

"Tomorrow night I'll do better," she said. "But I didn't want to waste time cooking when I could be over here with you. Why don't you go back to bed while I clean up the kitchen? Do you need help?"

He started to say no but thought better of it. "I need your help," he said. Gayle gave him her hand and helped him stand. He put an arm around her shoulder and leaned on her for support. He could stand alone, but he wanted the closeness. They walked slowly into the entry, and Landon turned toward the living room instead of the stairs.

"Let's sit in here for a few minutes," he said. "How were my classes?" he asked when they were settled on the couch. He kept his arm around her and pulled her closer.

"Lectures are going fine. We had a good discussion in American Presidency today. Marietta Wylie is a natural leader in there."

"Yes." Landon touched her cheek with his fingertips and traced her jaw line to her lips.

"I have missed you," he said. "I have missed touching you, kissing you."

"I've been with you every day for several hours. Have you forgotten?"

"A hospital room is not my idea of being together. I'm so glad to be home and have you here."

"I'm glad you're home, too. I've thanked God over and over that you're all right and home again."

With his fingers under her chin, he lifted her face so he could kiss her. The kiss was tender at first, but he wanted more. He leaned toward her and groaned.

"Landon, are you all right?"

He took a deep breath. "I'm fine now. I moved wrong."

"I thought it was a pretty good move," she said and chuckled. "Come on, you're going to bed. You've overdone it. And I want you well and taking your classes back before Randy Pressman makes it to class. And I hope that's not tomorrow."

She helped him upstairs.

"Do you need more water?" she asked after he was tucked in. She lifted his water pitcher and gauged it was half full.

"No, I'm fine."

"Okay. If you need me, I'll be in your study. I need to get back to Binford's text."

"Wouldn't you rather sit here and talk to me?" He patted the edge of the bed.

"Yes, I would. However, I must prepare for tomorrow's class."

"You've been burning both ends of the candle. And for me. I appreciate it, Gayle."

"Good. Then get well so I can go back to my normal job and you can get back into the classroom." She leaned down and kissed him before she walked downstairs.

A moment later he heard the doorbell followed by several voices in the hall. He distinguished Clark's voice among the din. A stampede on the stairs announced the entire basketball team from the church league.

"Hey, Dr. Windsor, we won tonight. A real squeaker. We needed you as guard. Benny did it, but—"

"I did good," Benny defended himself. "Made five points."

"Sounds good to me," Landon said.

Seven young men paraded into his bedroom and shrank the size of the room.

"Where's Clark?"

"He's downstairs talking to Gayle," Benny said. "What a looker. You'd better watch out. Could get some competition."

"From Clark?" Landon asked, feeling threatened.

"From everybody," Benny said. The team laughed.

Landon obtained a play-by-play from the guys before they left for their dorms. Clark and Gayle took their place in his room.

"I'm going home," Gayle announced. "If you don't mind, I'll take Binford with me," she patted the textbook she held. "We're getting to be good friends."

"You have to go now?" Landon asked.

"You're in good hands. Clark, if you need anything in the night, I'm only three houses away."

"I'll walk you down," Clark said.

Again Gayle leaned down and kissed Landon before she left. He could hear their voices downstairs and wondered what they were saying.

He closed his eyes. He was tired of being sick. Tired of having no energy. Tired of Clark talking to Gayle.

"Are you ready for bed?" He opened his eyes as Clark came back into the room.

"No, I'm not sleepy," Landon said. "Just tired. I've

taken good health for granted."

Clark nodded and sat down in the upholstered chair across the room. "We all do. Only when something goes wrong do we appreciate what we have. That Gayle is really something," he said, changing the subject.

"Yes, she is." Landon agreed and felt a sudden stab of jealousy. "Leave her alone."

eleven

Life wasn't going the way Landon wanted it. Gayle didn't come over before she went to work Thursday morning, although she called from the office to make sure the baby-sitting schedule was in place for the day.

"Clark left around eight-thirty. He has a nine-o'clock class. Kit's here now. Tom is coming this afternoon." Landon hit his head with the palm of his hand. "I forgot to give you the key to my office. Tom was going to pick up some files for me."

"I have your key, Landon. I still have all your keys. I drove your car home Sunday night, and I've been working in your study each night. I meant to return them yesterday."

"No, that's good you have them. Let Tom in the office when he drops by. He'll be here all afternoon, so Clark is rearranging the sitter schedule." Landon cleared his throat. "I told him tomorrow is the last day I'll need anyone. You'll be around all weekend. Right?" He held his breath until she answered.

"Of course, I'll be around. And by then you can stay alone at night. Richard's still on for tonight, and tomorrow night Clark will be back."

Yes, Clark would be back, Landon thought after he

144

finished talking to Gayle. He should never have snapped at him, for Clark had lectured him about trusting their friendship and love. And the upshot of the conversation was that Landon would be one lucky guy if Gayle continued to see him. And if she fell in love with him, well, according to Clark, Landon should thank God everyday for her.

And he did. First thing every morning, he talked to God and thanked Him for bringing Gayle into his life. With every passing day she became more important to him. If only he knew what secret she kept. If only she trusted him enough to confide in him. He also prayed for patience so he wouldn't ask questions that she would refuse to answer.

Landon covered his incision with plastic wrap and tape and took the first shower he'd had since Saturday. Although he was refreshed, the exertion wore him out. He took a two hour morning nap and rested before Tom arrived for their afternoon work session.

"At last," Landon said. He sat at the table in his study with questionnaires spread out in front of him. He had read each one as they had come in. A governor was his obvious choice for a Senate candidate, but he checked each one carefully in case a dynamic leader was just getting into the political arena. "I need to work. Accomplish something."

"How are we going to sort these?" Tom asked.

"We need a candidate who's known across his state already," Landon said, hoping to lead Tom to his own conclusion. "What sort of person would that be?"

"Someone who's already held an office. Not a newcomer to the scene. A state senator would have a wide constituency. Hey, we should follow someone who's been elected by the entire state. The governor or secretary of state."

"I agree," Landon said. "Governor would be the better known of those two. Let's start sorting these questionnaires by current office held."

Landon stayed seated while Tom reached across the table and sorted papers, moving stacks that had become too high.

"We have thirty-three U.S. Senate races and twelve of the candidates are currently governors," Tom stated. "That's a high percentage."

"How many candidates have filed at this time?"

"One hundred thirty-one in both parties. One Republican race has eight candidates in the primary. One hundred fourteen have returned the questionnaires."

"Okay. Let's look at the twelve governors. Before we can make decisions, we need more information." Landon moved to his desk and turned on his computer.

"We'll compile a bibliography of magazine articles about the candidates." He pushed a few buttons, and his computer dialed the library's number. After a few more gyrations on the computer, he was looking at the periodical guide on screen.

"You'll have to do the footwork," Landon told Tom. He input the name of New Hampshire's governor and watched the computer list articles. He pushed the print page button, and the printer noisily spit out a page. Landon input three others, then turned the machine over to Tom.

"I'm going to lie on the couch and review these." Landon took the computer printouts and their corresponding questionnaires into the living room.

Almost an hour later, Tom brought in the rest of them.

"Some governors don't have many articles," he said.

"That's what we want to find out. The fewer articles, the less visible to voters in other states. We want a candidate who will win, who has attracted national attention as a governor, and who is popular in his own state. If we get really lucky, we'll pick a man who will be President of the United States in another ten or fifteen years. That would insure that the book would stay in print a long time."

"Are you serious?" Tom asked.

"Although governors have been elected to the highest office, and we have no better example than our own former governor Clinton, usually presidential candidates are Washington insiders. They come from Capitol Hill. And usually from the Senate." Landon warmed to a favorite opinion of his. "Kennedy, Johnson, Nixon, Ford. Of course, Carter and Reagan were governors who skipped the Senate and went straight to the White House. I think the trend will be to go back to those who have had some experience on the federal level. We might be picking a future president."

"Wow," Tom said. "You want me to get all these articles?"

"Please. Do you have any time tomorrow to bring them by? Or could you leave them with Gayle?"

"If we're through for the day, I can go to the library now and get them. I'll drop them off tomorrow morning on my way to class, and I can be back here after three."

With that plan, Tom left Landon as soon as Jesse Hill reported for duty, and Gayle relieved Jesse shortly before five.

"I froze this lasagna last Sunday since we didn't get to have dinner. It'll bake in no time," she said, sticking it in the oven. "A salad, french bread. Anything special you'd like for dessert?"

"Dinner sounds wonderful," he said. And it was. He laid down on the couch while dinner cooked, then sat and held Gayle through a movie on TV. Richard arrived before it was over and watched the last of the movie with them.

"I'm out of here," Gayle said. "I should have been reviewing notes. It was a slow day at the office, so I've read through them once."

"You'll do fine," Landon said. "My students probably prefer you to me."

"Some of them do," Richard said. "I've heard talk in the halls. It's the male half that have no loyalty to old Dr. Windsor."

"I've got to get back to work," Landon said. "I should be able to take over on Monday after I see the doctor."

Tom delivered copies of magazine articles the next morning before eight. Richard had left and Benny had returned for his shift.

"Benny, don't you attend classes?" Landon asked him.

"Sure. But I don't have early ones or late ones. I arranged my schedule to fit my sleeping habits."

"Wise," Landon said. He covered his incision again and showered, then prepared for a full day of work in his study. Surely sitting up would not tire him out. He felt much stronger than he had the day before.

He settled back in his chair, glad that he could find a comfortable position so easily, and read four articles about the governor of Alabama. He made notes that he paper-clipped to the questionnaire and placed them in a file folder marked Alabama.

He picked up the articles on the governor of Kentucky. Gayle's state. He'd pay particular attention to this one and ask her opinion of the governor.

"Johnson?" he said.

"You want something, Dr. Windsor?" Benny called from the living room.

"No. Sorry, just talking out loud. Bad habit of mine."

He laughed to himself. Johnson was a more common surname than Smith or Jones. Just because they shared the same name, didn't mean Gayle was related to the governor. He turned the page of an article in Newsweek and stared at a picture of Governor Johnson and his daughter, Ginny.

She was looking at her father—with the same eyes that had looked at him.

He picked up his coffee cup, but his hand was shaking so badly, the hot liquid sloshed over the side. He grabbed a few tissues and mopped up the mess.

Gayle was Ginny Johnson. It fit together now. The Harvard education, her poise, her manner of speaking. He remembered seeing her talk to Arkansas's governor outside the library. Obviously she knew the governor. Probably had attended meetings with him.

Why was she here? And why couldn't she tell him about her family?

What was it she had said? She wanted time away from her family to start over. What had happened in Kentucky? There was the old boyfriend. That had to be the answer. His logical mind put two and two together and came up with four.

The boyfriend had hurt her. Probably used her for her position with the governor. It was an old story. Men used women to get power then tossed them aside. He could throttle him. No, if he hadn't treated Gayle badly, she wouldn't be here in Arkansas, bringing him dinner and caring for him.

How do I act around her? Do I tell her I know her secret? Landon asked himself.

The questionnaire. He flipped through the file until he found it. Attached was a letter from Virginia G. Johnson, the governor's aide, the governor's daughter. The governor did not wish to be followed through his campaign.

He remembered receiving that letter sometime in December. At the time he'd given it little thought. If he seriously considered the governor, he'd try him again. Sometimes assistants overstepped their boundaries and made decisions that candidates would reverse.

But this particular assistant knew Landon and had turned him down. *She didn't know me when she sent the letter,* Landon reminded himself. Perhaps she'd had a change of heart since then. She'd said she liked his writing. He reread the letter but found no reason for turning down his request.

He poured over the rest of the articles. There were eight. Gayle, or rather Ginny, was mentioned in five of them.

He turned on his computer and connected with the library again. He input Ginny's name, and the periodical index showed nine entries, the five which included her father and four of her own. She was more popular than the governor. *Redbook.* She had been profiled in *Redbook.* He read the abstract of the article. "Up-and-comer Ginny Johnson, daughter of Kentucky Governor Evert Johnson, sees public office as service to God and country."

He wanted to know more about her. Was it violating her trust to pursue it? He'd promised not to ask questions; he hadn't said anything about reading magazine articles.

Or newspapers. He'd bet the Kentucky newspapers were full of her. He pulled up the screen that catalogued newspapers and found only one Kentucky newspaper listed. But he found twenty-four articles in it about her in the last year alone. He printed the entries, then disconnected with the library.

He needed help, and he didn't think he could ask Tom. Landon dialed the reference librarian and asked for a favor. She'd heard of his operation and was glad to help him with his research since he couldn't get around yet.

Not only did she agree to get the newspaper and magazine articles for him, she volunteered to call a friend at the University of Kentucky and get information from other newspapers that they indexed. And she'd get it to him as soon as possible. Landon hung up with a satisfied feeling.

He read through the articles on the other governors. He would rank them Kentucky, Ohio, and Maine, but he'd listen to what Tom had to say once he had read them, too.

Kentucky wasn't a contender, though. Ginny Johnson had turned him down, and Gayle Johnson would feel used if he pursued her father. Landon would not jeopardize his relationship with her. Kentucky was out.

He removed that file from the stack on his desk and set it aside. He reevaluated the rest. Ohio, Maine, and California. Top three, but it wouldn't hurt to draft new letters to send to the twelve, make that eleven, governors. Each one might have convincing arguments for why he should be chosen. News changed daily. Some late-breaking story he wasn't aware of could change the complexion of the race.

Landon climbed upstairs, wondering if he would ever climb the stairs without holding onto the banister. Although he stretched out on his bed for over an hour, Landon never closed his eyes, but stared at the ceiling.

Gayle Johnson was Ginny Johnson. Ginny was Gayle. He had thought he knew Gayle. Now there was another personality thrown in, as if she were twins.

"Dear Lord, help me convince her that I love her for herself and not for who her father is," he prayed. His prayer came from his heart, and it took him a moment to realize he had said the L word.

Did he love Gayle? Yes, he admitted, he did. He had met her just a month ago, and he was in love. Head over heels in love. They had spent a great deal of time together and had packed more into that month than if they had dated every Saturday for a year.

She had read his galleys, they had gone to church, played racquetball, visited with friends. He had cooked for her. She had cooked for him. He may not know her background, but he knew Gayle and he loved her.

But did he know Ginny? How could he meet her without telling Gayle he knew the truth. And he didn't want to do that. He wanted her to trust him enough to tell him.

When Tom arrived a little after three, Landon worked with him drafting a letter to send to the governors. While Tom read the articles, Landon went over his notes, making sure his top three choices remained the same.

"Take the governor folders home and rank your top three choices," Landon told him. "We'll compare on Monday. I should be back at school."

"Should I send out the letter?" Tom asked.

"If you have time. If not, maybe Gayle will do it at school. The quicker we make our final decision, the faster we can begin in-depth research into the background of our candidate."

Gayle arrived before Tom had gathered all his folders. Landon tried to remain calm and look at her as he always had. Did it matter to him that she was the governor's daughter? If he was being honest, he would have to admit that knowing who she was did affect his actions around her. If possible he wanted to impress her even more.

"Have you got everything, Tom?" Landon asked his assistant.

"Let me double check," he said and ducked back into Landon's study.

Landon took the opportunity to welcome Gayle home for the day. He leaned down and kissed her lightly on the lips.

"I've missed you," he said softly, then straightened as Tom came out of the study carrying the governor folders.

"I've got everything now," he said. "I'll check your office on Monday. If you're not there, I'll call."

"I'll be there," Landon assured him.

"We'll talk Monday," Gayle told Tom. "Bye now. How's your project coming?" she asked Landon in what he thought was an intense voice.

"We're narrowing the search. We've decided to find a governor who's running for the Senate. We want a personality who's witty, quotable, and in the news. That'll help the general marketability of the book, although I'm aiming at outside reading lists for political science classes, too."

"I'm sure your book will sell," Gayle said. "You have a good track record. What does your publisher say? Will they accept the manuscript?"

"They already have. The book's scheduled out the end of November. I'll write chapters as the campaign rolls along and get them to the editor as I finish each one. It's all timely material."

"You'll be a very busy man if you follow a politician around day and night. When will you write? While he sleeps?"

She would know about the rigors of campaigning, Landon thought. *One article had mentioned that she had campaigned for her father since she had first learned to talk.*

"It'll be a hectic sabbatical," he said.

"Have you considered following a woman?" Gayle asked.

"I considered it, but I understand a man's drive better, his shortcomings, his attitudes towards the road show, that sort of thing."

"Perhaps you understand it too well. Do you think you showed an unbalanced picture in your presentation of politicians in *Trends in American Politics*?"

So that was why she'd turned down his offer to follow her father's campaign. She'd thought he'd been unfair and was protecting her father from that sort of harassment.

"I tried to show a complete picture. Unfortunately, the good ol' boy system and the 'I'll scratch your back, you scratch mine' mentality has taken over a large segment of our politicians. I'm looking for a good Christian man to follow this time around to show the American people that while Christians aren't perfect, they try to do what's right."

"I see," Gayle said. "Speaking of politicians, would you

mind if Marta and Ted came over tomorrow afternoon to review Ted's campaign?"

"Be glad to have them."

"Thanks, Landon. Did I tell you I invited Clark for dinner? Since he's back on night duty, I thought he might get some reward."

"Gayle, I'm fine now. I don't need anyone around."

"I know. But I'd feel better if you had someone just one more night. Please?"

"All right. What's for dinner?"

"Enchiladas. One of my specialties. Wait till you taste them. You can grate cheese if you feel up to it."

Landon followed her into the kitchen and sat down at the table while she brought him utensils for the various jobs she assigned him. He grated cheese, chopped olives, slivered lettuce, and chopped an onion.

Clark arrived just as they were putting the final touches on the meal. Gayle poured glasses of iced tea, then brought the enchilada casserole to the table.

"I'll say grace," Landon volunteered and reached for his friends' hands.

"Dear Lord, we thank You for today and all the blessings You've given us. Please nourish this food to our bodies and let it make us all strong. And please help us learn how to trust one another. Amen."

He opened his eyes to find both Clark and Gayle staring at him.

"Pass the cheese, please," he said smoothly.

twelve

When was that Kentucky-Arkansas game? Landon scrounged around on his desk until he found the basketball schedule. February twenty-second. Two weeks.

Unless he missed his guess, Governor Johnson would not let a press opportunity pass, and their own governor would be present for the game, probably challenged to a basketball duel. Gayle would have to tell him about her father and Frank Lukens before then or have her entire past blow up in her face.

He stuffed the *Redbook* article with Frank's picture back in the manila envelope and continued through the other articles. The Kentucky newspaper articles, which had been faxed, enlightened him the most. Quotes from Ginny Johnson, sprinkled liberally throughout the articles, could have been spoken by Gayle Johnson. They were spoken by Gayle Johnson. The twin personalities were melting into one for Landon as he read on.

Virginia Gayle Johnson was one sharp woman. He was surprised that she could ever fall for some shark like Frank Lukens.

He finished the articles and tucked them back into the manila envelope and into a desk drawer. A twinge of guilt niggled at his mind. Was he deceiving Gayle by checking

157

on her background?

Gayle rang his doorbell at ten-thirty the next morning and waved the newspaper at him when he opened the door.

"What did you think?" she asked.

"Scott Banks looks like a candidate without a platform, whose only method of campaigning is mud-slinging. Although this is a negative campaign tactic, I think Ted might come out of it just fine."

"Me, too," Gayle said. "Ready to go?"

She drove Landon to the campus church. The congregation fussed over him as he took a chair on the aisle. Several other professors shook his hand and said they had missed him at school. The students who had baby-sat, especially Benny, sported a proprietary air, as if they had been personally responsible for Landon's return to health. Gayle sat beside him and answered many of the questions directed his way from three or four ongoing conversations.

Clark Rossiter walked to the front of the large room. The seats quickly filled and a hush fell over the crowd. He started the service with a prayer thanking God for returning Landon to their fold.

At the end of the prayer, Landon stood and thanked the congregation for their help and prayers and thoughts and cards and flowers and visits during his illness.

"It is a humbling experience to know what good friends I have," he said. "Thank you all."

The group cheered. Gayle had never witnessed that sort of rousing welcome in a church before. More accustomed to the pomp and circumstance of a large church, she welcomed the openness of the members.

After a couple musical numbers from Southern Hospitality, Clark addressed the crowd.

"Through Landon's illness, I've found lots of Christian principles that we as a congregation have followed. Certainly that of service to each other applies here. Just as Jesus served people, we must serve others, too. In this instance, we have helped Landon, and it was not help that was asked for. When I mentioned to several of you that Landon was coming home from the hospital and might need some help, the response was overwhelming. If we had used all the volunteers to stay with Landon, we'd have had a party at his house around the clock. I commend you all for your service and for exhibiting true friendship.

"As Christians we strive to live a life that Jesus would have lived. Sometimes it's difficult and we need help. Sometimes we doubt those friends we have trusted. And that is a human characteristic. But who we cannot doubt is God. We can trust that He will work out our human frailties and lead us to a righteous life."

Landon squirmed in his chair. Was Clark directing this sermon strictly to him? He had doubted Clark and been jealous of his time with Gayle.

"Friends are those who help us when we need it, listen when we need to be heard, share our sorrows, and share our laughter and turn to us when they need help, too. This last week I have seen friends in action, and it has warmed my heart.

"I looked up a quote I've always liked. Dinah Maria

Mulock Craik wrote in *A Life for a Life:* 'Oh, the comfort, the inexpressible comfort of feeling safe with a person, having neither to weigh thoughts nor measure words, but pouring them all right out, just as they are, chaff and grain together, certain that a faithful hand will take and sift them, keep what is worth keeping, and then with the breath of kindness blow the rest away.'

"We trust our friends, and so we should. We trust them with our lives, we trust them with our children, we trust them with our secrets. For trust and friendship go hand in hand. Our ultimate trust, of course, is in God's love and in His understanding and in His Word."

Gayle squirmed in her chair. Was Clark aiming this sermon at her? She viewed Landon as a dear, dear friend, and she hoped he became even more than that. She loved him. But was she willing to trust him with her secret? It was dishonest to keep her past from him.

"We'll continue with our study of the Epistles of Paul," Clark said.

Gayle glanced at Landon and her attention shifted from Clark to him. He was staring straight ahead, and her gaze traced his profile as if she were running her finger across the contours of his face. She loved this man.

She bowed her head and silently prayed that she could trust him, too. Trust him to value the friendship they shared, to accept the love she gave, and to forgive her for deceiving him. For although she had not lied to him with words, her reluctance to confide her past was a silent way of lying.

Gayle lifted her head in surprise as Clark ended his sermon. Glancing at her watch, she discovered that he hadn't given an abbreviated talk, but she had been sharing her thoughts with God for the last twenty minutes.

She stood with the rest of the congregation and sang the doxology.

"Are you tired, Landon?" she asked, once they had shaken hands with Clark, filed out of the church, and were in her car.

"A little. But I'm glad I came."

"Me, too," Gayle said. "You definitely have a church family here that loves you."

"Yes. I'd like to do something for them, Gayle," he told her as she drove them back home.

"This isn't a religious idea," she said, "but I noticed you all don't have a ping pong table at the church. Where I come from, that's the big church game. Not basketball."

"We couldn't set one up and still have a basketball court," Landon said.

"True, but there are those kind that come in two parts and fold up, like card tables. You could store it in the back closet when it wasn't in use."

"That's a great idea. Think we'd need two of them? And a year's supply of ping pong balls? Are we going to your house or are you making me walk home?" he said when she pulled into her drive.

"I put a roast in the oven this morning which should be about ready. A change of place will do you good, especially if you're set on going to school tomorrow. Get you used to being out of your own house in small doses."

Gayle insisted Landon lie on the couch while she put the finishing touches on Sunday dinner. After a pleasant meal, she walked him back to his house as his afternoon exercise. The February sun warmed the air, all traces of snow were gone, but the trees were bare and the hope of spring still lay beneath the cold ground.

"I think I'll take a nap this afternoon," Landon said.

"Sounds like a good idea. I'll go back home and get caught up on my laundry and housekeeping. You'll call if you need me?"

"Yes. I'll call for a pizza later if you'll join me for supper," he said.

"Sure. Canadian bacon?"

He nodded.

"Okay. I need to go over your class notes for tomorrow. I'll spend a little time in your study when I come back. Anything you need before I go?"

"No, I'll be fine." He kissed her good-bye and headed up the stairs. As soon as he reached the top, he turned around and headed back down.

Lying on top of his desk was the file on Gayle's father, and in one drawer was the envelope filled with material about her. He didn't want her finding them.

He stashed the envelope at the back of a filing cabinet where she wouldn't be looking, then searched his desk for the file labeled Kentucky. It wasn't on his desk. With a moan he dropped to his knees and searched under the desk, thinking it might have been knocked off. Except for a rubber band, a pen, and two paper clips, the floor beneath his desk was clean.

He looked in his desk, through his files, and finally decided it had disappeared. Had Gayle taken it? No, if she had found it, she'd have confronted him.

Maybe Tom had stuck it somewhere. He phoned his graduate assistant and asked him.

"Oh, yeah. I found it on the desk when I went back in to make sure I had everything. Don't worry, I've got it with the others. I read them all and mailed letters to the governors yesterday." He sounded proud of his accomplishment.

"Did you write to Kentucky?"

"Yes. Don't worry, I got them all, and the Kentucky governor is one of my top three picks. We'll probably have replies within a week, so we can start moving forward on this project."

"Yes. Well, thank you, Tom. You've been a big help," Landon said, although he felt as if he'd been hit in the stomach, right on his appendix scar. "I'll see you tomorrow."

What was he going to do? He needed to calm down. Probably the governor would never see the letter. An assistant, perhaps the person who had taken Gayle's place, would read the letter, look for a file on the subject, see there was already a negative reply from Gayle, and fire back another refusal. Yes, that's what would happen.

But what if the governor did see it? Would he call Gayle and ask if she knew him? Would she figure out that he knew who she was?

"Please God, help me here. I trust you to lead me the way I should go with her," he prayed and felt a peace descend upon him. He climbed back up the stairs and took a long nap.

The next morning, Benny called for Landon precisely at eight o'clock.

"Hasn't this baby-sitting blown your sleep schedule?" Landon asked.

"You know, it had, but I'm getting more done." Benny sounded surprised as he backed his car out of the drive and drove to the doctor's office.

The doctor was forty-five minutes late coming into the examining room. Landon had paced the floor, waiting. Gayle was teaching his nine o'clock now and would probably have to teach his ten o'clock.

The doctor finally made it in, apologizing for the delay, and removed the staples that held Landon's incision together.

"This is healing nicely. You'll probably be sluggish for a few more weeks, then regain your normal energy level. If you have any trouble, call the office. Otherwise, I won't need to see you again."

Benny dropped Landon outside the history building, so that he didn't have the long walk from one of the student parking lots.

Landon's ten o'clock class had just begun. Instead of marching straight to the classroom, he dropped by the history office and found Dr. Webber sitting at

Gayle's desk.

"I'm back," Landon said.

"Welcome," Dr. Webber said and shook Landon's hand. "You're looking good."

"I feel fine. Thanks for letting Gayle take over my classes. I know that inconvenienced you," he said and waved his hand around to encompass the office.

"Everybody pitched in to help," he said. "That Gayle is a fine lecturer. Imagine a Harvard lawyer as my secretary. I know how to hire employees," he said with a laugh.

Landon chuckled and wondered what Dr. Webber would say if he knew his lawyer-secretary was also a governor's daughter. "I'm going to sit in on my class and see where I need to pick up on Wednesday."

Classroom two-fourteen had two doors, one at the front of the room and one at the back. Landon entered unobtrusively through the back door and took a seat in the back row. Only a few students turned around. Gayle had her back to him, writing on the blackboard.

She turned around and immediately focused on him. She smiled and continued with what she'd been saying. Her style was not that of a substitute reading notes. She knew her facts and she presented them in a dramatic and interesting manner.

"Beginning with George Washington's administration, we had a federal government where both parties were represented. Washington was a Federalist. Perhaps the strongest Federalist was Alexander Hamilton, first Secretary of the Treasury. He wanted uniform federal currency, instead of that which individual states issued. But the first Secretary of State, Thomas Jefferson, was a Republican. It's only natural that discussions would turn to arguments when men with wide political differences sat at the same table."

Gayle went on to discuss the differences in a clear manner that made note taking easy. She wrote important events and names on the blackboard, for emphasis and correct spelling. And she asked the students for interpretations of events.

"Dr. Windsor will lecture on Wednesday," she said at the end of the hour. "I appreciate your attention and cooperation during the last week. For Wednesday read chapters three and four and finish *The New Nation*. First test will be next Monday. Have blue books for the exam. Any questions?"

After telling them exactly which outside reading books and chapters in the text the test would cover, Gayle dismissed the class.

"You're an excellent speaker," Landon said, "and a born teacher." That didn't surprise him. After all, she'd been giving speeches all her life.

"Thanks. What did the doctor say?"

"Staples are out and I'm fine. He said take it easy for a while, which I will. I'm going to find a ride home after my two o'clock. Has Tom stopped in today?"

"I haven't seen him."

"If you do, would you send him to my office?"

By the end of the week, Landon was staying at school the entire day. Two ping pong tables had been delivered to the campus church. And by the first of the following week, the first of the governor letters had been answered.

"What about Ohio?" Tom asked. "He's anxious to be our candidate. And what about California? Such a big state has a lot of clout nationally."

"California's one of my choices. As soon as all the governors respond, we'll rank them again."

"What about all the other questionnaires?"

"As soon as we make our choice, we'll send letters to all the candidates advising them of our decision." He counted the letters on his desk. "We haven't heard from six governors. If we haven't heard in another few days, we'll call them. If the candidate doesn't want to be selected, we can't force him, and he'd be very uncooperative during the campaign. Stop by tomorrow after class and we'll see how we're doing then."

Landon filed the letters in their respective folders, then picked up the Kentucky file to reread. Yes, Governor Johnson would be his number one pick, but it would never happen. Upon reflection, he had fired a letter off to the governor, telling him that he was sorry to have bothered him with a follow-up letter, but his folder had gotten mixed in with the candidates he was considering, that he knew that the governor didn't want to be the subject of his book, and that he thanked him for his time. He also knew he wouldn't get a reply.

So Landon was stunned when Annie buzzed his phone

and told him he had a call from Kentucky on line two. He immediately glanced at his watch and saw that Gayle would be getting back from lunch anytime. He took a deep breath and picked up the phone.

"Landon Windsor," he answered the phone.

"Dr. Windsor, this is Wayne Harvest out of the governor's office in Frankfort. I have your letter informing us that you won't be considering Governor Johnson for your campaign book. Would you enlighten us on why you have eliminated him from the running?"

"It was my impression that the governor didn't want to be considered," Landon replied. "In December I received a letter from Virginia Johnson stating just that."

"I see. I wasn't aware that Ginny had made that decision. If the governor wishes to reverse that decision, would you consider him for your book?"

Landon's mind would have jumped at the chance to write about Governor Johnson, but his heart said no. "Although at this point he would be my first choice, other circumstances dictate that I not follow the governor's race."

"What circumstances?"

"I'm afraid I can't reveal those."

"And you won't change your mind?"

"No," Landon said. He would never jeopardize his relationship with Gayle by involving her family, especially her father. "But thank you for calling and for your interest."

He hung up the phone just as Gayle poked her head in

his office.

He glanced guiltily at her.

"Landon, would you like to watch the city council debate on television tonight? Seven o'clock, my house, popcorn."

"Can't pass up popcorn," Landon said. "You've decided not to attend?" Gayle had almost single-handedly set up the television debate between the four candidates.

"I think Ted would be more nervous with me there."

"Okay. I'll be there. And, Gayle, I picked up four tickets for Saturday's game. What time are your parents coming in?"

This time Gayle looked guiltily around the room.

fourteen

Gayle paced the floor, waiting for Landon. She'd made regular popcorn and caramel popcorn and carried both over to the coffee table and turned on the television.

She and Ted had gone over the issues until after midnight last night. He had rebuttals for every possible statement his opponents could make. But Gayle was experienced enough in these matters to know that something unexpected could occur.

Besides worrying about Ted's performance, the clock was ticking away the minutes until her parents arrival on Saturday morning. She had taken no action to solve her problem. She hadn't told her parents that she was living incognito, nor had she told Landon about her father.

What was she waiting on—a declaration of love? Yes, she admitted, that was exactly it. No matter how confident she felt that Landon loved her, she felt the same way as she did with the debate. Something unexpected could happen.

A knock on the door announced Landon. Gayle took his jacket and hung it on the coat tree.

"Wind has sure come up and cooled things off," Landon said after he had kissed her.

"How could it possibly be seventy degrees in February, anyway?" Gayle asked.

"There's an old saying. If you don't like the weather in the Ozarks, stick around another ten minutes and it'll change. Who knows what tomorrow will bring?"

"Yes, who knows?" Gayle didn't mean the weather, but her dilemma with Landon. So far the newspapers hadn't mentioned her father's impending visit, but she knew it was only a matter to time. *Only you know, God,* she prayed silently. *Please help me.*

"I got good seats for the game," Landon said. "Pretty high, but right in the middle. Since your folks are Kentuckians, I wanted to be impartial."

"That's considerate," Gayle said. "My dad's a basketball fan." *And he's also the governor,* she added in her mind. She wished she had the courage to say those words out loud.

The local news theme song came on the television.

"Is Ted prepared?" Landon asked.

Gayle switched her thoughts to the debate. "I think so. He's got every fact and figure we could find on the issues. He's speaking at Kiwanis tomorrow, and Thursday at Rotary. I thought we'd saturate the civic groups at one time, then mail the flyers and start the door to door campaign. Marta's organized walkers in every precinct."

"Have you finished?" he waved toward the table which was covered by computer printouts of registered voters in each precinct.

"Almost. I just lack updating two streets in our area. Only eight more weeks until the election. That last week will be our media blitz. I think he'll win," she said.

"I think he'll win," Gayle said again after the debate. She had taken notes while she watched the event. "He came across as the most informed candidate. He looked good on camera, and his speech sounded natural, as if he were talking to the neighbor next door."

"Yes, he looks like a winner," Landon agreed. "Congratulations. You've worked hard for him. He's a good candidate, but it takes more than that to win an election." He was giving her an opportunity to tell him about her past election experiences. Would she take it?

"Thanks. Ted's done the most work, of course. Well, I'm glad that's over. He'll call for my comments as soon as he gets home."

"Are you throwing me out?" Landon asked.

"Not exactly, but I'll be on the phone for awhile."

"That's okay. I've got work waiting for me at home. How about a racquetball game, Gayle? We haven't played in the longest time."

"Are you ready for that kind of exertion?" she asked.

Landon was glad to see the concern on her face. "I'm ready. I want to get back in shape. I'm playing Richard tomorrow after school. I'll check and see when we can get a court."

She agreed and he kissed her good night before walking out into the wind.

By Friday, Gayle was beside herself. She had prayed about her problem, she had cried about her problem, and she'd lost sleep about it, too. After their racquetball game, she would tell Landon the truth. Otherwise, he'd know the next day when her folks showed up for the game.

They wouldn't be using the tickets Landon had gone to a great deal of trouble to obtain. Gayle picked up the sports page again and read about her father and the Arkansas governor trading good-natured comments about the outcome of the game. The Arkansas governor would be providing tickets to this event, Gayle's mother had informed her when she'd called about their arrival time at the airport.

Gayle had to tell Landon that night. Her day zipped by as she dreaded their game and the conversation afterward.

She should have beaten Landon. He was slower than his usual quick pace and was winded early in the game. But her racquetball game reflected her lack of concentration.

"Good game," she said to Landon after he beat her by seven points. "Did I promise you dinner if I lost?"

"I don't think we mentioned it in words, but it's one of those understood things."

"Maybe we should vocalize the things we think are understood," Gayle said as they walked off the court.

"Does that mean you're not providing dinner?" Landon teased.

"I got all the fixings for subs, just in case," she said.

"I was going to order a pizza, just in case," he confided.

Back at Gayle's apartment, they each fixed a submarine sandwich and sat down at the round table to eat.

"I've been thinking about your remark," Landon said.

"What remark?"

"About us not vocalizing everything we think is understood between us. It dawned on me that I've never told you I love you. And you know I do."

Gayle stood up suddenly, knocking her chair over in her haste. "How can you say that so calmly?" she demanded.

Landon stood, too, and set her chair back on its legs. "I assumed you knew. I know you love me."

"Oh, you do, do you?" she asked, but she was all smiles.

"Yes, I do." Landon took her in his arms and kissed her. "You wouldn't kiss me like that, if you didn't love me. And I see it in your eyes."

Gayle pulled his head back down to hers and kissed him again. "I do love you. Very much."

"Now that we have that established, can we finish our sandwiches?" Landon asked with a chuckle.

"A romantic moment like this deserves candlelight and steak, not fix-your-own sub," Gayle said.

"It's the company that matters, not the food or the atmosphere," Landon said. "I thank God daily that I've found you."

"He hears the same prayer of thanksgiving from me," Gayle said. "He also hears my plea for help."

"Help?"

Gayle looked down at her hands for a long moment before she looked up into his eyes. "You're aware that I haven't told you about my past and why exactly I'm here in Arkansas. Oh, you guessed there was a man. But I didn't explain." She cleared her throat, ready to make a clean breast of things.

"My father is in a very influential position and Frank

courted me in order to gain political favor with my father. I didn't matter to him, only my connections. That hurt. I wanted to be known for myself, to prove that I was a good person who could make friends and take care of myself without using my father."

She paused and took a drink of iced tea. Landon remained quiet, willing her to go on.

"My father is Evert Johnson, governor of Kentucky. He's been in public service since I was small. I've campaigned for him and I worked in his administration before I came here."

Landon reached over and took her hand. She had finally made her confession, but he couldn't leave it at that. They were being honest with each other, a very necessary step in their relationship. He intended to marry her, and he wanted a clean conscience between husband and wife.

"I know," he said.

"You know?" Gayle said in a quiet voice. "You know?" she said louder this time.

"I found out while working on my book. I sent a questionnaire to him, which I'm sure you remember answering. That's why you had read my books. I didn't make the connection when I first met you. It was only later, after my operation, when I was working on the selection process, that I saw your picture with him in an article."

"You know all about me and my family?" Gayle asked.

"I read all the articles about your father and many about you. The *Redbook* article was impressive. Your dad is quite the politician. He'll win that Senate seat."

"I see. So, have you made your selection for your book?" she asked in a tight voice.

"Not yet. That depends on you. Your father is our number one choice."

"I want you to leave, Landon. Right now," Ginny Johnson said in an icy voice. If she had been hurt before by Frank, it was nothing to how she felt now. Before her heart had been broken in two. Now it was crushed into a million pieces.

"But, Gayle," Landon protested. "You don't understand."

"I understand all I need to know. And don't call me Gayle. I'm Ginny."

She walked to the door with her head held high, held the door open, and motioned him through it.

"When you regain your senses and are ready to listen to me, to trust me, we'll talk," he said in an angry voice and stomped out.

"I'm Ginny Johnson, the governor's daughter, and I have been used one more time," she said aloud. He wanted to follow her father's campaign, but she had turned him down. Now he wanted her to reconsider because of her feelings toward him. How could he do this to her? Her shoulders shook with her sobs.

"Oh, God. Why me? Why again?" she cried. Landon had said he loved her. But if he loved her, he wouldn't ask her to use her influence with her father.

She needed someone to hold her and let her cry out her anguish at betrayal. She needed someone to tell her it would be all right, that her heart would heal. She needed Landon to be that someone. She wanted his arms around her comforting her, telling her it had all been a mistake, that he wasn't trying to use her to get to her father.

After she had cried every tear, Gayle washed her face and reached for the phone. Marta. She'd understand.

The phone rang before her hand touched it. She recoiled. What if it was Landon?

She let it ring four times, then tentatively lifted the receiver to her ear.

"Hello?" she said.

"Hi, Ginny. We're looking forward to seeing you tomorrow," her father said.

"Good. For a second there I thought you were calling to cancel. I saw in the paper that you'll be sitting with Arkansas's governor. Having a mini-convention?" She forced a smile into her voice.

"We're going to beat the socks off those Razorbacks," he said. "The reason I called, Ginny. Do you know Dr. Landon J. Windsor?"

She took a deep breath. "Yes. He teaches in our department."

"He's writing a book," he began.

"Yes," she interrupted, "I know all about it."

"Then why has he eliminated me?"

"What?" she exclaimed.

"He told Wayne that he won't consider me, but won't tell him why. I understand you turned his request down in December, but Wayne read his books and thought he'd do a fair job."

"He told Wayne he wouldn't consider you?" She sat down hard on the couch.

"Yes. Can you find out why? Or arrange a meeting with Windsor so I can talk to him? Being in his book would be a political plum."

"I'll do what I can, Dad. I'll see you tomorrow morning. Bye now." She rang off quickly and took time to grab her coat before running to Landon's house. The rhythm of her footsteps said, He loves me, he loves me. He had said her father was the best candidate, but he had turned him down. Because of her. She had jumped to the wrong conclusion and wouldn't let him explain.

"God, please help me make it right between us."

No lights blazed from Landon's home, but she held her finger on the doorbell anyway. After a minute, she gave up and peeked in the garage window. His car was gone. Where could he be?

She walked slowly back home, wondering what to do next. Should she call around to his friends? If she found him, did she want to apologize over the phone? No, it would be best to see him in person.

She threw herself into a cleaning frenzy, getting her apartment ready for her parents' company. She baked cookies, then walked back to Landon's house. No lights, no car in the garage.

By midnight Landon still had not returned. Gayle walked back home in the dark after her fifth trip to his house.

"Dear God," she began her nightly talk after she'd crawled in bed. "I'm always asking for help. You've given me Landon and I've throw him away because of my own insecurities. Please help me again. I must find him and explain before it's too late."

She slept and woke early the next morning. As soon as she had showered and dressed, she made the trek to Landon's again.

Still no answer. She peeked into the garage. Still no car. Had he stayed out all night? Where could he be? Had something happened to him?

Back at her apartment she paced, then reached for the phone. Washington General said he wasn't a patient. As soon as it was a decent hour, she'd call Richard and Clark.

She waited until eight-thirty and thought that was late enough, even though it was Saturday morning. She chose Clark first and hit pay dirt.

"Landon spent the night here, but he left about a half hour ago," he said.

"I accused him of some terrible things," Gayle said. "I've got to find him."

"Don't worry, Gayle. God will show you the way. And Landon will be receptive when you find him. He loves you."

"I know," she said and hung up.

He had left a half hour ago. Another walk to Landon's revealed he hadn't gone straight home. She had to pick up her parents at the airport in fifteen minutes, so she needed to leave. But oh, she hated to go, leaving things unsettled between them.

She could have stayed at home and waited. Her parents' plane was thirty-seven minutes late. She had watched every one of them tick off the big clock on the wall in the disembarking area.

Just as her parents walked across the tarmac, Gayle spotted the newspaper reporter who had written about Scott Banks' false claims against Ted. She didn't want to be front page news, but she didn't know how to avoid it. She was surprised there were no television cameras but knew they would be in full force that evening when the two governors met for the game.

"Hi, honey," her mother greeted her and gave her a big hug. "It seems like six months instead of six weeks since I've seen you. You look good."

"Thanks, Mom. Hi, Dad." She accepted a bear hug from her dad and saw the flash of a camera. It would probably be front page. She was back in the fish bowl again.

"Come on. I'm anxious for you to see where I live," she said and hoped she could hustle them out of the airport and into her car before the reporter could stop them.

"Governor Johnson." The reporter stared at Gayle, who was collecting bags, before giving his full attention to her father. He asked about the game and the meeting with Arkansas's politicians.

"And this is your lovely wife?" the reporter asked.

"Yes. And my daughter, Ginny," he said.

"Ginny Gayle Johnson," he said and smiled slyly at her. "We've met."

"Remember, Dad, I'm helping Ted Novak with his campaign."

"And doing a great job," the reporter said. "He's the front runner right now."

Governor Johnson patted his daughter on the arm. "She knows how to run a campaign. She's helped me for years."

Gayle could see the wheels turning in the reporter's head and made a quick excuse for them to continue to the car.

"Did you ask Windsor about his book?" Governor Johnson asked as Gayle drove them toward her apartment.

"There's a long answer that goes with that question. Why don't I tell you over coffee?"

As soon as they were settled in her apartment, Governor Johnson repeated his question.

Gayle took a deep breath and made a clean confession—from being known by her middle name to how she felt about Landon and why she had ordered him out of her house.

"And now I can't find him. But even if I could, Dad, I wouldn't ask him to use you in his book. That smacks too closely of using him for what he can do for me. I've been on the receiving end of that, and it doesn't feel good."

"I understand, Ginny. When you've been in public life as long as I have, you learn to be a careful judge of character. I never liked Frank, but since you seemed to, I didn't make my feelings known. Sounds like Landon Windsor is a different sort of man."

"He's a kind, honorable Christian man. I just hope he can forgive me for doubting him."

"Do you think he's home now?" her mother asked.

"I don't know."

"Why don't you find out?" she suggested. "I'm going to finish the mystery story I was reading on the plane, and your father needs to go over some papers." She made a shooing gesture with her hand. "Scoot on out of here and give us a little time alone."

Gayle hugged her mother. "If he's home, I'll be a few minutes. If he's not, I'll be right back." She grabbed a jacket and darted outside and down the sidewalk to Landon's.

This time she peeked into the garage before climbing the steps to the front porch. His car was there. Her hand shook as she reached for the doorbell.

"Dear Lord, give me the courage to face him."

She pushed the bell and waited only a few seconds before he opened the door.

They stared at each other for a long moment before Landon held out his arms and Gayle rushed into his embrace.

"I'm so sorry," she said. "I'm so sorry."

"Me, too," Landon said and hugged her close. "I should have handled it differently. I knew you were hurt before when Frank used you to get to your father. I didn't realize that what I said sounded like the same thing. Clark pointed that out to me. I don't blame you for lashing out."

"I should have trusted you enough to listen to your explanation. I tried and convicted you without listening to your testimony. Some lawyer I am."

Landon chuckled and led her inside to his study.

"You're a fine lawyer. What you did was let your heart rule your head for once, and that's not necessarily a bad thing."

He pulled out the chair behind his desk and motioned for her to sit down.

"I want everything between us to be open. No misunderstandings." He crossed to the file cabinet and extracted the thick manila envelope and handed it to her. He had added articles from the librarian's friend in Kentucky. They had only clarified his mental picture of Ginny Johnson.

"Since you wouldn't tell me about yourself, I read about you."

Gayle dumped the contents onto the desk and sorted through them.

"I suppose a political scientist steeped in research would naturally seek the truth," she said. "I would have done the same thing if our positions were reversed."

Landon breathed a sigh of relief and sat down on the other side of the desk.

"About using your father in the book. What I would have explained last night is that I won't use him unless you want me to."

"I know. Dad told me you had turned him down."

"I wouldn't do anything to hurt you."

Gayle smiled at him. "Whether you choose my father is between you and Dad. It would be unfair of me to bias you."

"He's an ideal candidate. He's a popular governor, his

party is in power in the state, and he should be elected." He reached across the desk for her hand. "Another plus for following his campaign would be traveling with my wife. You could help your father one final time, and we could be together. But when we come back to Fayetteville, I think you should take a shot at being the lawyer you want to be. Maybe practice a year or two until the children come, then take time off to get them in school before you defend justice again."

"You've got it all worked out."

"Yes. Do you like the plan?"

"I love it, and I love you."

Landon quickly skirted the desk and gathered her in his arms. He kissed her with all the gentleness of love. Several kisses later, Gayle pulled away.

"My parents are at my apartment. Are you ready to meet them?"

"Sure. I want to ask your father for his daughter's hand in marriage."

"You'll have to be prepared for what it means to marry the governor's daughter. My picture will probably be on the front page of the newspaper tomorrow." She told him about the reporter at the airport.

"There are many sides to all of us. Ginny Johnson will be in the paper tomorrow and for many days to come. But Gayle Johnson will be here." He touched his heart. "And you will always be Gayle to me."

epilogue

The bride, glowing in the tradition of love, followed her matron of honor, Marta Novak, down the long aisle of the church, where cascades of flowers adorned every pew.

Gayle tugged on her father's arm to slow him down. She had marveled that the governor, always at ease in front of cameras and large crowds, today had hands that were cold and clammy.

"This day's hard on your old man," he had told her before their long walk began.

"Don't worry, Dad. I'll always be your daughter, even if I am Landon's wife."

"And you love him, daughter?"

"With all my heart."

The governor had smiled at his only daughter and had wiped a tear from his eye.

Now Gayle looked ahead at Landon waiting in front of the altar. Richard stood beside him, and Clark, resplendent in formal robes Gayle knew he had never worn in the campus church, waited with Bible in hand to begin the ceremony.

As soon as the couple pledged their love in front of God and their assembled friends and family, Marta lifted the veil from Gayle's face.

Landon kissed his new wife and she kissed him back with all the love inside her.

He triumphantly led her down the aisle and outside into the bright sunlight. Still cameras clicked and television cameras hummed as reporters covered the event of the year.

One reporter stuck a microphone in Landon's face. "How does it feel to be married to the governor's daughter?" he asked.

"Wonderful," Landon said and quickly handed Gayle into the waiting car that would take them to the rose garden reception at the Governor's Mansion.

"You'll get used to that," Gayle said. "There's very little privacy. Everything we do will be news for awhile."

"I can take it," Landon assured her. "I managed when the press descended on you at the Kentucky-Arkansas ball game and at Ted's victory party. And I managed last night after the rehearsal. The public wants to know about you, and I understand that. I have my system for separating your public and private lives. Ginny Johnson is loved by the people of Kentucky. But Gayle Windsor is loved by me."

A Letter To Our Readers

Dear Reader:

In order that we might better contribute to your reading enjoyment, we would appreciate your taking a few minutes to respond to the following questions. When completed, please return to the following:

Karen Carroll, Editor
Heartsong Presents
P.O. Box 719
Uhrichsville, Ohio 44683

1. Did you enjoy reading *The Governor's Daughter*?
   ☐ Very much. I would like to see more books
       by this author!
   ☐ Moderately
       I would have enjoyed it more if _____

   _____

2. Are you a member of *Heartsong Presents*? Yes   No
   If no, where did you purchase this book? _____

   _____

3. What influenced your decision to purchase
   this book? (Circle those that apply.)

Cover	Back cover copy
Title	Friends
Publicity	Other _____

4. On a scale from 1 (poor) to 10 (superior), please rate the following elements.

     ___Heroine   ___Plot

     ___Hero   ___Inspirational theme

     ___Setting   ___Secondary characters

5. What settings would you like to see covered in *Heartsong Presents* books?

_____

_____

6. What are some inspirational themes you would like to see treated in future books?_____

_____

_____

7. Would you be interested in reading other *Heartsong Presents* titles?   Yes   No

8. Please circle your age range:

| Under 18 | 18-24 | 25-34 |
| 35-45 | 46-55 | Over 55 |

9. How many hours per week do you read? _____

Name _____

Occupation _____

Address _____

City _____ State _____ Zip _____

add a little *MYSTERY* to your romance

TWO GREAT INSPIRATIONAL ROMANCES WITH JUST A TOUCH OF MYSTERY
BY MARLENE J. CHASE

_____*The Other Side of Silence*—Anna Durham finds a purpose for living in the eyes of a needy child and a reason to love in the eyes of a lonely physician...but first the silence of secrets must be broken. HP6 BHSB-07 $2.95.

_____*This Trembling Cup*—A respite on a plush Wisconsin resort may just be the thing for Angie Carlson's burn-out—or just the beginning of a devious plot unraveling and the promise of love. HP5 BHSB-05 $2.95.

Inspirational Romance at its Best from one of America's Favorite Authors!

FOUR HISTORICAL ROMANCES
BY COLLEEN L. REECE

___ *A Torch for Trinity*—When Trinity Mason sacrifices her teaching ambitions for a one-room school, her life—and Will Thatcher's—will never be the same. HP1 BHSB-01 $2.95

___*Candleshine*-A sequel to *A Torch for Trinity*—With the onslaught of World War II, Candleshine Thatcher dedicates her life to nursing, and then her heart to a brave Marine lieutenant. HP7 BHSB-06 $2.95

___*Wildflower Harvest*—Ivy Ann and Laurel were often mistaken for each other...was it too late to tell one man the truth? HP2 BHSB-02 $2.95

___ *Desert Rose*-A sequel to *Wildflower Harvest*—When Rose Birchfield falls in love with one of Michael's letters, and then with a cowboy named Mike, no one is more confused than Rose herself. HP8 BHSB-08 $2.95

LOVE A GREAT LOVE STORY?

Introducing Heartsong Presents —
Your Inspirational Book Club

Heartsong Presents Christian romance reader's service will provide you with four never before published romance titles every month! In fact, your books will be mailed to you at the same time advance copies are sent to book reviewers. You'll preview each of these new and unabridged books before they are released to the general public.

These books are filled with the kind of stories you have been longing for—stories of courtship, chivalry, honor, and virtue. Strong characters and riveting plot lines will make you want to read on and on. Romance is not dead, and each of these romantic tales will remind you that Christian faith is still the vital ingredient in an intimate relationship filled with true love and honest devotion.

Sign up today to receive your first set. Send no money now. We'll bill you only $9.97 post-paid with your shipment. Then every month you'll automatically receive the latest four "hot off the press" titles for the same low post-paid price of $9.97. That's a savings of 50% off the $4.95 cover price. When you consider the exaggerated shipping charges of other book clubs, your savings are even greater!

THERE IS NO RISK—you may cancel at any time without obligation. And if you aren't completely satisfied with any selection, return it for an immediate refund.

TO JOIN, just complete the coupon below, mail it today, and get ready for hours of wholesome entertainment.

Now you can curl up, relax, and enjoy some great reading full of the warmhearted spirit of romance.